MW00514473

Eton Mess Massacre

Steve Higgs

Text Copyright © 2022 Steven J Higgs

Publisher: Steve Higgs

The right of Steve Higgs to be identified as author of the Work has been asserted by him in accordance with the Copyright, Designs and Patents Act 1988

All rights reserved.

The book is copyright material and must not be copied, reproduced, transferred, distributed, leased, licensed or publicly performed or used in any way except as specifically permitted in writing by the publishers, as allowed under the terms and conditions under which it was purchased or as strictly permitted by applicable copyright law. Any unauthorised distribution or use of this text may be a direct infringement of the author's and publisher's rights and those responsible may be liable in law accordingly.

'Eton Mess Massacre' is a work of fiction. Names, characters, businesses, organisations, places, events, and incidents either are the product of the author's imagination or are used fictitiously. Any resemblance to actual persons, living, dead or undead, events or locations is entirely coincidental.

Contents

Prologue — Cat and Mouse

His lungs were searing from the effort of running. He hadn't run like this since he was at school almost three decades ago and he had been not only much younger, but distinctly lighter too.

A voice echoed through the steel structure of the factory.

"Come along, Joseph. Where is it that you think you're going? There's no way out."

Had there been enough air in his lungs to do so, Joseph would have spat a response at his tormentor. Instead, he paused to heave in a lungful of oxygen as lights started to dance in front of his eyes, and pushed on, climbing as quickly and quietly as he could in his bid to escape.

Adrenaline raging through his blood stream was making him feel both sick and faint at the same time. Were they going to kill him if they caught him? Surely not. The idea seemed just too ridiculous. Of course, he had no idea who *they* were, but they showed up less than fifteen minutes after he accessed the firm's encrypted files, and they somehow knew who he was and even which office to find him in.

Had it not been deathly silent in the factory, he might never have heard them coming. As it was, he only narrowly slipped out of the chief executive's office before they arrived.

It was Jessica, of course. Jessica who had made him suspicious. Not that he was attempting to blame her for his current predicament, but had she not approached him with her concerns, he might have gone the rest of his life without ever finding himself being chased the way he was.

"Joseph," the unfamiliar voice echoed through the structure again. It had an odd quality to it, and he couldn't decide if it belonged to a man or a woman. "Joseph you are only prolonging the inevitable. I promise that it will be quite painless."

The lack of emotion in the voice was terrifying, and the words being spoken cleared away any lingering doubt that he might be permitted to go back to how things were.

Frantically looking around, Joseph searched for a way to escape. When he had started running, he believed it was a simple case of getting to a door. Okay, so it was night outside and the carpark would be empty, but he'd left his car unlocked as was his habit and felt confident that once he was in it no power on earth could stop him. He would happily drive through the factory's ancient wrought iron gates if he got the chance.

However, his escape route had been cut off, a tall, dark figure appearing in the walkway before him as he fled. There was no thought that he could muscle his way through or overpower the man blocking his path. Whoever it was, he had to be well over six feet tall and his flat top hair style reminded Joseph of *Ivan Drago* from the *Rocky* movies. He wasn't about to pick a fight with *Ivan Drago*.

He didn't get to see the man's face but there were now at least two people after him in the dark of the factory and his only advantage was that he knew the place intimately. It was at that point he chose to go vertical, clambering silently onto the walkways running above and between the machines. Hunkering down for a moment behind the boxing machine, he cursed himself for being so foolhardy.

Naturally, when he set out to access the secure files, he'd told himself he was being brave. Sneaking into the factory at night with a stolen password to access a restricted area of the company's server, he'd known there would be trouble if he got caught. If he survived to blow the whistle, he knew that was what people would say about him.

But only if Jessica's outlandish concerns were true. He'd managed to access the files, but the chance to examine them was snatched away by the arrival of the people now pursuing him through the dark. He didn't need to see the files though to know everything Jessica believed had to be true. The very fact that his life was in danger stood as testament enough that everything Jessica claimed was accurate.

Staying as still as he possibly could and breathing through his nose even though his aching lungs demanded he supplied them with more oxygen, Joseph watched from above.

The factory was silent, the machines all dormant until the morning when the early shift would arrive. Not even the maintenance team were here at this time of night. During the day his movements would be undetectable among the background noise of a busy working environment. In the still of the night, Joseph was convinced they could hear his heart beating.

A minute ticked by. Then two.

Despite what his pursuer had said, it appeared that Joseph had indeed managed to lose them. It was a temporary victory at best though, for as soon as he attempted to move, they would reacquire his position and if he merely stayed where he was, they would eventually find him.

Terrified by his lack of options, Joseph knew that he had to make a break for the door. Six yards above the shop floor, on a steel mesh walkway intended solely for maintenance purposes, he could make it almost all the way across the factory in the shadows above their heads.

Almost.

When he got to the split and sort, he would have to jump from one walkway to the next. How far was it? Joseph closed his eyes and tried to picture the gap in his head.

Was the gap eight feet or ten? Was it more than that?

How far could he jump anyway?

He hadn't been up onto the walkways in years, not since he got promoted to the management team at least, so it had been a long time since he had seen it other than from the ground. He was certain there was a fire exit at this level somewhere, but in the dark, in spite of believing he knew the factory like the back of his hand, he had no idea how to find it.

Slipping off his shoes, in a moment of clear thinking, Joseph slowly rose to his feet. The steel mesh bit into the soft soles of his feet, but it was nothing more than an inconvenience he could suffer now that he had a possible plan in his head.

Taking aim, he drew back his right arm and launched a shoe across the factory. It was swallowed by the darkness no sooner than it had left his hand, but he heard when it connected with the stainless-steel side of the Packer.

He waited a two count to confirm that his attempt at a distraction had worked, and when he heard quiet footsteps tracking away from him below, he began moving.

Wincing and cursing as he walked as fast as he could across the painful steel mesh, he felt buoyed by how quickly and quietly he was now moving.

The voice punctuated the silence again, this time sounding distinctly displeased.

"Joseph, I am becoming irritated. Where are you?"

Whispering quietly to himself, Joseph replied, "On my way to the police." His phone was in the car, or they would already be on their way. In his pocket where his phone ought to be was a portable data drive. The files he'd accessed were on it now and all he had to do was get out and give it to Jessica. She would do the rest.

It was her data drive; one she'd given him specifically to copy the files if he was able to get in.

The gap was coming up, and though he was nervous about jumping it in the dark, he had convinced himself that it was going to be easier than his memory imagined.

It was lighter in this part of the factory where one or two of the old skylights had been replaced. They were clean and let the moonlight filter through which could not be said of the others which were covered in decades of grime and moss.

Joseph was thankful for it until he realised that if he could see his surroundings, his pursuers could probably see him. Panicking, he took out the data drive, hefted it momentarily as he argued with himself, then stashed it where it would be found by one of the maintenance guys next time they came this way. It was safer than getting caught with it. Maybe he could bargain with them if they captured him; convince them to let him go if he told them where it was. He hadn't really seen what was on it after all; they turned up right after he opened the first file.

When in the next second a shot rang out like a thunderclap, he swore loudly, ducked automatically, and lost his footing.

Bored with the game of cat and mouse, the cat had chosen to see how steely the mouse's nerves were.

Not very it proved, as her decision to shoot a hole in the ceiling high above her head instantly revealed her quarry's position. The small calibre bullet would leave a miniscule hole that would be noticed at some point in the future when it rained. By then it would not matter.

Swinging around to pinpoint Joseph's location, Chrissy Mullins heard his terrified exclamation, and the wet thud that followed it.

Standing just a few feet away, her colleague, Kasper, asked, "Did you hear that? You think he's all right?"

She rolled her eyes, wondering if she could have picked a less intelligent henchman. It was as if lifting weights reduced brain power in a trade-off that balanced itself out.

Keeping the gun in her right hand, she took out her torch and proceeded to look for where Joseph might have landed. That she couldn't hear him, she took to be a bad sign.

The boss wanted to question him. That was his first instruction. His accountants had security systems set up to monitor the encrypted files and were highly motivated to ensure they reacted fast if anyone were to ever access them without the proper permissions. That had just happened, and she was paid a fat retainer to be ready to move whenever Mr Crumley called.

There was someone snooping where they should not be, and her task was to capture them. She would have hurt him a little, obviously.

Mostly for her own pleasure, but also because it would make him more pliable before she handed him over. He didn't know it, but Joseph Lawrence was dead the moment he logged in tonight. If he was working alone, it would end there, but she already knew that he wouldn't be. They never were.

It took almost twenty minutes to find him because he had fallen inside one of the machines. She didn't know what it was and did not care. What she cared about was that it was not possible to extract him.

She explained this in a phone call to her employer. He wasn't happy, but at least he didn't argue with her opinion on the subject.

Joseph Lawrence would be found in the morning when they turned the machine on. It would look like an unfortunate accident, and in many ways that was what it was. There would be an investigation, and the police would question why he was in the factory at night and why he had been up on the maintenance walkways without his shoes on. They wouldn't find any answers though and Mr Walsh knew to keep his mouth shut.

Placing the gun back into the holster underneath her left armpit, she slapped an arm on her idiot henchman's muscular chest.

"We're leaving. We have evidence to plant."

Kasper grunted a response, the sound of his footsteps in her wake enough to reassure her that he was following.

A check of her watch confirmed how little time she had before the body was likely to be found. Between now and then, she needed to create a false trail that would lead the cops to believe Joseph Lawrence was involved in something sordid. It would divert their attention, muddy the waters, and provide a tangible explanation for his death.

A suicide, she decided, was too clichéd. Better to leave his death looking slightly suspicious.

Leaving the building, her thoughts were divided between covering up the unfortunate mess that had become Joseph Lawrence and her continuing concern that he had to be working with someone else.

Dirty Old Man

The news article seemed to jump off the page. Albert hadn't even intended to read it, but now he couldn't do anything but, even though the newspaper was in the hands of a young woman sitting opposite him on the train.

He had to skew his head to the right a little to be able to see the words as the page curved where it sat with the bottom edge resting on the woman's lap.

"I rather hope you are reading my newspaper and not trying to look up my skirt," she commented abruptly.

Startled, Albert jerked his body upright, his cheeks filling with colour like a child caught raiding the cookie jar. Passengers on the other side of the carriage were looking his way and frowning their contempt. Eyes wide, Albert tried to explain his behaviour only to be rudely cut off before he could begin to speak.

"Just my luck," the woman snapped. "There are seats available on the train for once and I manage to sit opposite a dirty old man." She was already getting up and turning around to fetch her bag from the overhead luggage shelf.

Stuttering and trying not to mumble, Albert said, "No, I was reading the paper, I swear. There's an article about a winning chef being killed. I have ... um, special interest in the subject." His explanation sounded weak because it was. He was on the trail of a master criminal that few in the world even believed to exist, but he couldn't say all that in the time he'd been given.

The young woman looped the strap of her bag over her head so it fell diagonally across her body. She was in her late twenties, Albert's retired cop brain supplied – twenty-eight perhaps. Her auburn hair was pulled into a ponytail and would be just about shoulder length if set free. She had dark brown eyes and a serious case of freckles that gave her face a summer-kissed look.

Dressed in office wear and elegant heels, she looked like a business-woman returning from a meeting. Albert figured it had to be returning rather than impending due to the time of day – it was after four and the sun was setting.

Hopelessly scrambling to think of something else to say, Albert caught a final disparaging look from the woman before she walked away without a further word – she didn't think he was worth the effort.

Albert's dog, an oversized German Shepherd and former police dog called Rex Harrison, shot his human a look.

"Were you hoping to mate with her? Because that didn't seem to go very well. I can give you some tips if you like."

Aware that the dog was staring at him, Albert reached out with his right hand to scratch the fur under Rex's left ear. He couldn't understand what the dog had to say – it was just noises to Albert's ears, but he also found himself quite often willing to believe that Rex was trying to communicate.

Embarrassed by what had happened, and steadfastly ignoring the faces still watching him, Albert looked out the window. The denuded deciduous trees of the Kent countryside flashed by outside as the train hurtled toward London. It was late afternoon on a Saturday in mid-autumn, and he was on his way to Cornwall.

There he hoped to pick up the trail of a master criminal, the Gastrothief, as he had come to call him, and he had just enough time to get there on the last train.

When a few minutes had passed and the eyes on him had drifted away, Albert leaned forward to collect the newspaper. The woman had abandoned it when she left her seat, but it had felt wrong to immediately fall upon the thing he wanted, illogical though he accepted that was.

Flattening the paper out, Albert started the article again.

It was the headline that first grabbed his attention: *Eton Mess Champion Dies*. Albert's eyes were glued to the page as he read.

ETON MESS MASSACRE

Joseph Lawrence of Eton, the health and safety manager at Wallace's of Eton, the primary supplier of ready-made Eton Mess puddings to the entire nation, was found on Friday morning when factory workers discovered a blockage in the boxing machine.

Albert was so hooked by the story that he stopped moving for long enough that Rex got concerned and nudged his human's hand with his nose. Albert barely noticed. His mind was racing, and he could not shift the feeling that he was reading about yet another Gastrothief incident.

Absentmindedly stroking Rex's head, Albert murmured, "It's just like the vineyard."

Just days ago, following a lead his eldest son had identified, Albert arrived back in his home county of Kent where a leading wine connoisseur had fallen to his death. Several of the vineyard's staff had gone missing and both vines, wine, and equipment had been stolen in a bizarre crime only Albert's theory could explain.

Was Joseph Lawrence's death the same thing? Outwardly it fit the pattern.

For the last few months, Albert had been touring the British Isles on a culinary mission. He couldn't cook, that was the crux of it. His wife, Petunia, had always been the one in the kitchen, so a year to the day of her passing, the seventy-eight-year-old retired senior police detective packed a small suitcase and backpack, clipped Rex to his lead, and walked to the nearest train station.

It had been pretty much murder and mayhem everywhere he stopped ever since. Only when some of the random crimes began to show similarities did he choose to look for other events that could feasibly be connected. Then, like a lightbulb coming on, he found a picture that linked one strange crime to another. After that, if one was prepared to suspend disbelief, the reality of a master criminal operating in the background was obvious.

His theory had very recently led him to Kent where he had almost caught two agents of the Gastrothief. Now he was being blamed for the mess they made and was on the run from the police who wanted him for questioning, and from the Gastrothief's agents who knew his name and home address.

In Cornwall he hoped to catch them in the act. He could clear his name, prove his theory, and get the full might of the nation's police to find the man behind it all.

But what about Eton? He was going to Cornwall because he'd found one of the agent's phones. An email on it showed a reservation at a B&B in the coastal village of Looe for tomorrow night. He had a whole day to get to Cornwall.

Biting his lip as he wrestled with his options, he accepted what he already knew he was going to do and nodded his head.

"Rex," Albert made eye contact his dog, "there's been a change of plan."

Coincidence

A lighting from the train at Waterloo east, Albert followed the throng of foot traffic as people climbed the stairs to leave the platform behind. Like a snake in motion, the crowd wove through a raised tunnel with very few electing to take the exits onto the streets outside. They were heading for the main Waterloo station, a giant hub offering services right across the South and Southwest of England.

Where most took the escalator to get down into the station, Albert elected to use the stairs in deference to Rex.

Ahead of them, a bank of huge electronic screens showed the next services due to depart from every platform. Once he was close enough to read them, Albert paused.

"Eton. Why can I not see Eton?" After several minutes of squinting and searching, Albert accepted defeat and went to look for someone to ask.

That task proved more difficult than he expected, for the ticket machines were electronic, and the booths with people in them had long queues.

When finally he spotted a uniform going past, he had to be fast to catch him.

"Platform six, mate," replied the skinny tattooed youth beneath the oversized Southeast Network Rail hat.

Albert looked away, staring up at the screens to see if he could confirm what he was being told, and looked back only to find that the young gentleman had already walked away; whatever business he had seemingly more pressing than helping a passenger. How times had changed since Albert was a lad.

Finally finding the listing for platform six - the bank of screens were not displayed in order as one might have expected - Albert discovered, much to his horror, that the train was due to depart at precisely the time his watch was currently displaying.

Cursing under his breath, for he rather fancied a trip to the gentlemen's' restroom, and perhaps a refreshing beverage, he instead got his feet in gear.

"No time to lose, Rex."

Rex frowned at his human. "Where is it we're going now? I could do with a visit to somewhere outside if you catch my drift. Also, my belly thinks it's dinner o'clock. And my belly is never wrong."

Albert gave a gentle tug on his lead to get Rex moving and hustled over to platform six where he discovered a guard looking very much like he was about to set the train on its way.

Spotting the old man hurrying as he was, the guard generously opened the very last door on the train, before whistling and signalling just as Albert was clambering aboard.

The train began moving with a gentle jolt before Albert could find his seat, but he was on board, and a few moments later, when the London landscape began to flash by, he was opening his backpack to find Rex's dinner.

Rex wasted no time in tucking into his chow, a can of gravy-soaked meaty chunks, but remarked, "This is only going to add to my need to go for a walk somewhere private. I hope this isn't going to be a long journey."

Questioning his sanity at the sudden change in plan - it was already evening on a Saturday and he was heading to Eton with nowhere to stay, Albert took out his phone, and called a friend.

Wing Commander Roy Hope was one of those chaps that you wanted by your side if things got dicey. Just the right side of eighty years old, he'd been retired for longer than he'd served, but the attitude and spirit of the British service person had never left his soul.

Together with his wife, Beverly, Roy lived opposite Albert in their quiet village of East Malling.

"Albert!" he trumpeted upon answering his phone. "How is everything? Are you in *you know where* yet? Are the *you know who's* there already?"

It amused Albert that his neighbour had immediately fallen into the role of secret agent upon joining him for an adventure in Whitstable a few days ago. Everything was already 'mum's the word' and speaking in code.

Not wanting to put him off, Albert replied in kind, "I've had to divert from *you know where*. I believe I have found another incident at the hands of *you know who's* agents."

"Golly!"

"Yes," Albert agreed. "It necessitates this call, in fact. I'll need accommodation for this evening. Is that something you can fix for me, Roy?"

Albert could almost hear his friend and neighbour saluting when he replied, "Absolutely. Just for the night? You'd better text me the destination, rather than saying it out loud where ears might hear. Make sure you delete the message afterwards though, old boy."

Albert grinned, but said, "Yes. Just for the night, I think. I have a date to keep tomorrow, but a day should be enough to find out if there is anything to gain from my impromptu stop off."

"Leave it with me then, Albert. I shall not let you down. When I have something, I'll forward you the booking by email."

They ended the call without any unnecessary pleasantries; Roy was insistent on the need for brevity as well - less words meant less chance of discovery. Albert imagined it had to be something Roy had learned during his days in the Royal Air Force, but couldn't really see how it applied to his current situation. He was alone on a train on his way to Eton. Even if agents of the Gastrothief had any idea where he had been for the last twenty-four hours, they couldn't possibly know where he was now.

Albert sent his destination via text message and then dutifully deleted the thread of messages before placing his phone back in his inside coat pocket and looking through the window at the lights of the buildings beyond.

Rex had focused on nothing but devouring his evening meal since getting onto the train. Now that his bowl was thoroughly clean, he gave himself a moment to examine the various scents and smells filling the air of the carriage.

It took him less than a second to be surprised when he recognised one of them. Turning around, he lifted his nose and sniffed again, sampling the air, and holding it in his nasal passage for scrutiny.

There was a human on board, a female whose scent he recognised. It took him a short while to figure it out because it was such a random connection, but Rex was quite certain he was able to smell the woman they'd been sitting opposite earlier.

Did that mean something? Unlike his human, Rex was not able to visualise the concept of a master criminal. Nor was he able to see connections between the places they had been and the mysteries they had solved. To him they were each separate with the confusing exception of meeting the same people a few times.

There had been two of them just days ago and they were clearly criminals, Rex had no trouble understanding that concept. Trained to be a police dog and then fired, in his opinion, for being too good at it, he was never happier than when he had someone bad to chase.

Using his nose, he tracked and found the perpetrators behind each crime while Albert and other humans were still using their eyeballs to look for clues. It used to really bother him that they refused to employ their strongest sense, but had come to understand that they were simply incapable.

That did not mean that his human was without use and the old man had proved himself valuable on several occasions. More than anything though, Rex just liked working with him.

The old man was fun.

Concluding that the presence of the woman from earlier signified nothing untoward, Rex spent a few minutes sifting and sampling the rest of the smells available to him. He wasn't doing it for any particular reason; it was merely a way of passing the time in much the same way that his human was now staring into the darkness outside the train.

Albert's eyes were getting tired, and he was fighting against the desire to let them close. He didn't want to fall asleep and run the risk of overshooting his stop. They were twenty minutes into a journey that would take a little less than an hour - he could stay awake for that long.

Listening to his stomach rumble, Albert lamented the lack of time the connecting trains had given him. Thankful there was a restroom on board the train, he whiled away the time thinking about what he might find for dinner, and it wasn't long before Windsor and Eton station was the next one on the line.

Rex was beginning to huff and puff with his need to be off the train and was really rather glad when his human stood up and began gathering their things together.

Sensing what Rex needed, Albert wasted no time in exiting the train.

"Tickets, please." The exit wasn't blocked by a physical barrier, but a short man with a sharp nose was barring Albert's path, nevertheless.

Reaching for the ticket in his trouser pocket, Albert's heart sunk – he didn't have a ticket for the journey he'd just made.

"Tickets, please," the short man in the Southeast Network Rail uniform repeated.

"Yes," Albert held out the ticket he did have. "I've made a somewhat unintended detour."

The man's face, which was stern to start with, turned ugly, and without a word, he directed Albert to the ticket booth set against one wall and the equally stern-faced woman sitting inside it.

Feeling like he'd been caught trying to dodge the fare, even though he hadn't, he apologised to Rex and fumbled for his wallet.

"Where did you board the train?" the woman in the booth demanded, her tone not exactly accusatory, but far from friendly.

"Waterloo."

While his human was doing whatever it was he felt it necessary to do, Rex fretted about his need to 'water' something. He was going to 'water' the wall in front of the booth if this took much longer.

The scent of the woman from the previous train caught in his nose, twitching his head around just in time to see her sweep by and out into the early evening air.

His lead was jerked as Albert went around him, encouraging Rex to hurry up if he wanted to do 'his business'.

The lady behind the counter had been kind enough to give Albert a pensioner's discount on his ticket and directions to the B&B Roy had booked for him. Albert couldn't book his own accommodation because the police would be tracking his cards. It was a very basic version of flying under the radar, but there was no mammoth manhunt for him despite the arrest warrant, and he was confident the simple precaution of using a false name would be enough to stop the police, or anyone else, from finding him.

Now clear of the station, Albert looked around for somewhere he could take Rex. His own bathroom needs were taken care of on board the train, but poor Rex had been forced to wait, so it came as no surprise when upon exiting the station, his dog took a sharp left turn and almost pulled Albert over in his haste to get to a lamppost.

Waiting for Rex to finish, Albert let his gaze rove until it found its way to a lone woman walking away from the station. He wouldn't normally allow his eyes to linger, but watching her walk down the street, her heels clicking on the pavement, a frown formed.

His eyebrows knitted together above his nose as his brain delivered the message that he was looking at the woman he'd been sitting opposite during his train ride into London from Kent earlier.

Her auburn hair and smart business attire were unmistakable as she passed beneath a streetlamp.

Seeing her again so many miles and more than an hour from their earlier interaction was nothing more than a simple coincidence; the type of coincidence that Albert would allow, for he was very much of the opinion that coincidences never occurred during police work. Taking a step to the left to avoid the stream of liquid now making its way towards his shoes, he dismissed her, but as he did so, movement caught his eye.

A large figure had just peeled out of an alleyway to follow the woman with the auburn hair. Albert watched for a moment, the part of his brain that contained so many years of experience as a police officer twitching in the background as it debated whether it was really seeing what it thought it was.

The man, dressed all in black and sporting a flat top haircut, had to be well over six feet tall - it was difficult to judge accurately from such a distance. Albert was familiar with the hairstyle but hadn't seen anyone sporting it since the early nineties.

Rex finished what he was doing and placed his right rear paw back onto the pavement. He still needed to find some grass, but had faith that his human understood basic needs. Wherever it was they were going next, Rex assumed it would be a public house or perhaps their accommodation for the night - typically those two things could be one and the same place - it was bound to include a stop off at a public park area along the way.

He noticed however that his human was standing unusually still and was staring up the road into the distance. Rex lifted his nose to give a tentative sniff. There was a rubbish bin approximately eight yards away; it had a distinctive odour that was a blend of foodstuffs and ageing rotting waste plus the discarded ends from cigarettes where a separate receptacle for them sat within the lid.

His sensitive nose also detected rodent tracks nearby, the individual scents of more than two dozen dogs who had marked the lamp post and other stationary objects in the last day, and on the breeze, a vague trace of the woman who had been sitting opposite his human on the train earlier.

None of that added up to much so far as Rex was concerned, and using his eyes revealed nothing else that he felt should hold his human's attention.

Nudging the old man's leg with his nose, Rex asked, "What are we doing? Shall we get some dinner?" That he had recently eaten did not enter the equation. He wasn't hungry, but since when was that a good reason to not eat? It was very much the old man's routine to find a meal at around this time of the day and that generally meant some scraps to clear up for Rex and possibly a drink of something.

Unable to strip his eyes from what he was seeing, Albert drew in a slow breath through his nose, held it for a two count, and made a decision.

"Come along, Rex. I believe there is about to be a mugging."

Sic 'em, Rex!

With Rex at his side, Albert crossed the street and began walking. His pace was fast because the lady with the auburn hair was about to reach a cross street and would vanish from sight if she turned a corner.

The man in black was no more than half a dozen yards behind her, keeping pace but doing nothing more than that. That nothing had happened yet caused Albert to question his own judgement. Was he seeing crimes where none existed now? The tendrils of doubt invading his mind prevented him from doing anything more than continuing to keep pace and watch from the other side of the street.

He didn't want to get too close and felt sure he didn't need to. If the man produced a weapon or chose to rush the woman he was following, Albert knew Rex could cover the ground between them in just a few seconds.

As he feared, the lady with the auburn hair turned the corner. Unconsciously holding his breath, Albert watched to see what the man would do. If the man carried straight on, Albert felt sure he would laugh at himself, but at the same time be thankful for his overactive imagination.

If, however, the man turned right and followed the woman, Albert would know he was right and quicken his pace to get closer.

Still forty yards behind the man when he also turned the corner and also disappeared from sight, Albert muttered an expletive that would have earned him a stern scowl from his late wife, Petunia, had she heard it.

Now all but running to catch up, Albert still couldn't be sure that the impending attack wasn't just his imagination working overtime. Skulking in an alleyway was not a crime. Nor, for that matter, was dressing all in black.

Albert reached the corner, his heart in his mouth until he saw both the man and the woman still walking along the pavement ahead of him. The distance between them was roughly the same it had been, which many would consider to be good news. However, Albert saw yet another indication that things were not as they should be.

The lady was wearing heels and had to be at least a foot shorter than the man. His stride pattern thus would be significantly longer, and it was knowledge born of experience that told Albert the man was going deliberately slow so that he did not overtake his intended target.

Target. The word echoed inside Albert's head. It could easily be substituted for another word: victim.

His concern was growing for the crime of mugging, or street theft, was generally one of swift, opportunistic ambush. If snatching her purse and jewellery was the man's intention, he would have done it already despite the populated area they were in.

Furthermore, the man did not fit the demographic for an opportunistic thief, and that could mean that his intentions were something else entirely less savoury.

Albert continued to argue with himself because intervening before anything happened would likely draw the police - he needed to avoid them at all costs. So he followed, Rex at his side and looking as if they were out having a pleasant evening walk.

Rex wasn't paying any attention whatsoever to the two humans ahead of them. He could see no reason to be interested in them. His sole focus was in finding somewhere his human would let him off the lead.

They had been walking for several minutes, the streets around them filled with terraced houses and no green spots at all. However, he could smell a grassy area ahead. Sycamore trees, a pond, and the cursed scent of a dozen squirrels filled his nostrils and quickened his pace.

"Whoa there, Boy." Albert tried to slow Rex down, but his dog was determined to go faster. The one thing Albert didn't want to do was draw attention to the fact that he was now behind the man with the flat top hair. Knowing his dog as he did, Albert began to question whether Rex could tell that something was about to happen.

With that thought in mind, he allowed the gap to close and calculated they would catch up to the flat top in less than a minute.

Except that didn't happen at all. The moment they passed beyond the houses, and a small park opened up on their right, Rex took the path leading into it.

"Dammit, Rex, this is not a good time. Can't you hold it?"

Rex understood the question and had a simple response. "How about if I give it to you to hold? How about that? We'll see what your opinion is then."

Grimacing as he was forced to wait while Rex adopted a hunched position, Albert ducked to look through the trees. The click, click of the woman's heels on the pavement marked her location as she got farther and farther away from him. The man was there still too, but so long as Albert could hear her feet, he would know nothing had happened to her.

Which is why it jolted him into action when the sound of her footsteps began to fade away.

Crouching to look under the lower branches of the trees bordering the edge of the park and weaving about to make sure his line of sight was not obscured, Albert struggled to spot the man.

Had something happened already?

Guiltily, when Rex was finished, Albert ignored the task of clearing up after him, and rather than walk through the park as he would on any other occasion, he reversed the direction to get back onto the pavement.

To his great horror, he discovered that neither the lady with the auburn hair nor the man with flat top were anywhere in sight.

He spat another curse word and moved as fast as his ageing legs would allow. At seventy-eight, his athletic days were far behind him. So far behind him, in fact, that sometimes they seemed as if perhaps they were just something he imagined.

Pushing his pace with an excited dog tugging him along, Albert's knees started hurting before he'd covered ten yards. Doing his best to ignore the unpleasant and unwelcome sensation, Albert struggled onward thinking his efforts would be so much easier if he wasn't carrying a suitcase.

Passing the entrance to another street on the left-hand side of the road, Albert caught sight of precisely what he didn't want to see and knew why he was no longer able to hear the woman's high heels.

She was stationary.

The man with the flat top had raised his hood – a classic preparation for attack - and was closing in on her position. He wasn't running; his pace remained unchanged, but the lady with the auburn hair appeared oblivious to the threat he presented.

When another, smaller black-clad person appeared beyond the victim – another man but a short one this time - Albert knew there was no time left to lose.

Sandwiched between two figures, both of whom wore hoods to shroud their faces, the lady's attention was on the contents of her handbag. She had it hooked on her right forearm, the handles spread so she could peer inside.

With a triumphant expression Albert could see from all the way down the street, she yanked a large bunch of keys from their hiding place.

Albert had no idea what the couple intended, yet every sense in his body screamed for him to prevent whatever it was or forever regret not doing so. As a police officer, he would have needed to wait for them to act. Such restrictions no longer applied.

Perhaps it was that he was already wanted by the police that drove him to be less cautious than he otherwise might, but with a yell of, "Hey!" to get their attention, he grabbed Rex's collar, unclipped his lead, and growled, "Sic 'em, Boy!"

Rex's eyebrows shot for the sky, and twisting his head upwards to check with his human, he said, "Sorry, what? Are you saying it's chase and bite time?"

Albert had expected his dog to explode into action as he always did given the slightest provocation. More often than not in such circumstances, it was all Albert could do to keep his dog under control until it was time to attack. Now the big dopey creature was just staring at him.

Flaring his eyes, Albert jerked an arm in the direction of the three humans some fifty yards down the street, and raising his voice once more, yelled, "The two men in the hoods, Rex! Get them!"

Rex didn't understand quite what was going on, but he had a command to follow and playing chase and bite was one of his favourite things in the world to do.

He was confused though for his human had commanded him to attack the two men and there was only one. He sniffed again, checking to be sure he was right.

The man was the closest; they'd been following him for some time. Just beyond him was the lady from the train. Then there was a new person and *her* scent confused him. It was both male and female he decided.

Each human's smell is created by a combination of sweat, scented products, their race and gender and a bunch of other minor factors, but usually the scented products are feminine or masculine. Rex didn't really understand humanity's desire to alter their natural smell, but the third person in the street could be either a man or a woman and he genuinely wasn't sure which it was.

Either way, he had a job to do, and it wasn't going to get done if he just stood around.

All three had turned to look in his direction as Rex bounded forward, hitting full speed less than ten yards from his standing start. With his eyes, Rex scanned for weapons. He knew well enough that humans could wield guns and knives and even blunt instruments such as bats that would be hard for him to defeat.

He couldn't see anything like that immediately, and his speed across the ground was such that it was already too late for him to abort his attack.

The man had begun moving, his first stuttering, nervous steps, quickly turning into a run. With Rex bearing down on him, he drew level with the first woman, the one Rex perceived to be that which needed to be protected, and grabbing her roughly, threw her into Rex's path.

She squealed with shock as she fell, the unexpected manhandling catching her completely by surprise.

Whether deliberate or serendipitous, it was a well-timed tactic, for Rex was going altogether too fast to make a hard turn, there was no time to whip beneath the woman's body before she hit the ground, and attempting to leap over her was likely to result in a mid-air collision.

With no choice but to brake as hard as he could, Rex dug his claws into the pavement, and did his best to stop.

The unfortunate woman slammed into the hard stone slabs, the air rushing from her lungs in a painful whoosh of exhalation that ended her fear-induced shriek. Beyond her, Rex could see the two humans running away and having come almost to a complete stop, he gave a grunt of effort, and took off after them once more.

Moving even faster than he had been before, Albert huffed and puffed along the road behind Rex. He'd seen the tall man take off and had been forced to watch as the intended victim was sent flying. The attackers, having anticipated where the woman was going, or perhaps coordinating their approach by use of phone messages, had effectively pinned her between them. It was Albert's belief that they were moments away from springing their trap.

Wishing once more that he wasn't carrying his luggage, he pushed his body harder to get to the victim.

Reaching full speed again, Rex was once more in pursuit. The two humans had gone between the cars, sprinting diagonally down the street, but Rex's hope that they might simply be attempting to get away from him was dashed when he saw the lights of a car flash.

He was a lot faster than any human, but even so he knew he wasn't going to catch them before they were safely in their car.

The smaller of the two, the one Rex felt sure was a woman, reached it first, hurdling the rear end to land on the pavement whereupon she ripped the driver's door open and shot inside. The man reached the passenger side no more than a second and a half behind her, and just as the engine roared into life.

Rex was moving as fast as he could go; his body a blur of rippling muscle sheathed in a fur coat. What he could do against a car was limited, but that wasn't going to stop him trying.

Back at the site of the attack, the victim had rolled onto her front and was attempting to get to her feet when Albert arrived.

"Are you hurt?" he asked, dumping his suitcase, but keeping his backpack over his shoulders in case the need to move fast wasn't over. Wheezing in a deep breath, Albert added, "You're safe now. Rex has chased them off, I think."

He said the words just as he heard a car's engine start and the squeal of rubber as whoever was driving it floored the accelerator. Albert jerked his head up, and unable to see anything, gripped the bonnet of the car next to him so he could lever himself into a better position.

"Rex!" he bellowed with all his might. The dog was racing after the car, pointlessly giving chase when there was no hope he would be able to keep up.

Rex had given chase to motorised vehicles before and knew it was less futile than others might be willing to believe. Success came down to how far the vehicle was going to go.

Identifying the unique smell of a vehicle's exhaust gases was a skill he'd taught himself during his time as a police dog. He could follow a vehicle given the correct set of circumstances which generally came down to how many other cars there were about and how far the target vehicle went. In the quiet suburb in which Rex found himself, it was not unrealistic to expect the exhaust smell to linger on the air for several minutes after the car had passed any given point. It would dissipate over time, even with no other cars around and no breeze, yet when he heard his human shouting for him, he chose to let the car go.

Largely, this was because he still wasn't sure why he was chasing them. Had they been attacking the third human, the woman from the train? He hadn't seen them do so, and though the man threw her to the ground, he only did so when Rex gave chase.

Panting from the exertion, Rex slowed his run, stopped, gave the air one last sniff, and started back towards his human.

It took several attempts for Albert to convince the woman to stay where she was on the pavement. She wanted to get up, which was completely natural, but it was clear that she had hit her head; a trickle of blood from her hairline, and a small but obvious lump gave Albert cause for concern.

Convinced that the danger had passed, he shucked his backpack and placed it next to his suitcase. Down on his knees on the cold pavement, he raised his head once more to check that Rex really was coming back towards him, before offering the young lady a smile.

"I'm Albert," he said, attempting to impart friendliness and warmth.

"Jessica," the woman replied, holding a hand to the wound on her head and wincing. "Jessica Fletcher."

A smile instantly creased Albert's face. "Jessica Fletcher?"

Hearing the amusement in his voice, Jessica huffed out a tired breath.

"Yes, just like Angela Lansbury in *Murder, She Wrote*. I could kill my parents." Hastily changing the subject, she said, "Thank you for coming to check on me." Tutting, she removed her hand from her head, noted the small amount of blood on her fingers, and looked at Albert for the first time.

Her face froze.

Anticipating what was coming, Albert said, "I was sitting opposite you on the train into Waterloo East."

A deep and suspicious frown now dominated Jessica's features, and her eyes were angry when she replied.

"Have you been following me? You're the one who tried to look up my skirt. Who are you?"

Reaching into his jacket to take out his wallet, Albert did his best to show that he was no threat.

"I can assure you I was reading the paper as I claimed at the time. The article on the front page took my interest, though I apologise, for it was rude of me to simply read it in the manner that I did. I had no idea that you were coming here, or who you are for that matter. Nor did I have any intention or expectation of ever seeing you again. If I can convince you to believe all of that, you will still want to know how it is that I come to be here at this precise moment. The answer is that I used to be a senior detective in the police, and I spotted a man following you. I know the signs, you see, and suspected from the moment that I saw him, that his intentions were criminal."

Rex arrived back at Albert's side, circling around behind him before taking a seat to the old man's left. The woman from the train was bleeding; Rex had picked up the coppery tang from her wound not long after he ceased pursuing the car and was now unsure what the protocol might be.

Was he supposed to lick it? He would if it were a dog in his pack, but humans could be quite odd about their sense of hygiene.

Jessica's face crinkled in confusion.

"What man? Who are we talking about? You mean the man who knocked me over when your dog chased him?" What Jessica didn't say as her accusing eyes bored into the old man's, was that she was worried he might be right.

She hadn't seen the man, hadn't even been aware that he was there, but recent events in her life gave rise to concern that she might be a target. Had the old man just saved her? If so, what fate had she inadvertently avoided?

Albert struggled to find words. "Um." It was an impossible situation. He'd stepped in to save her from attack, but because the attack never happened, she blamed him for her injury.

Jessica was taking her time to get back to sitting up straight. Her head was pounding, and she felt a little woozy. Even with her head spinning, she was able to add things up and there was a chance the old man could be of use. She was going to have to play it carefully; she couldn't give him reason to doubt her story or scare him off. He couldn't know the truth, but if she got this right, his interest in what happened to Joseph might be a tool she could use.

Planning her next sentence carefully, she said, "I'm sorry. That was rude of me. I'm sure you were only trying to help."

Albert couldn't think of anything to say in reply.

Surprising Albert, Jessica pushed herself upright and announced, "I need to get going. Thank you again for being a good citizen."

Using one hand in the air to balance herself, she pushed off the ground with the other.

Albert couldn't work out why she wasn't more concerned about the couple who ran away, but couldn't challenge her on it. Whatever her reasons were, they were none of his business and he needed to get up off the ground. His knees were hurting, and if he stayed down there much longer the cold was going to get into his bones. Taking a firm grip around Rex's neck so he could use him as an anchor point to haul himself upwards, Albert rose to his feet, then offered Jessica a hand.

"Are you sure you are all right?" he asked, feeling guilty that he wasn't offering to see her all the way home.

She took his offered hand and allowed him to help her up. She wasn't entirely convinced by his explanation, but equally she didn't believe that he had deliberately followed her all the way here from Waterloo East and could see the paper he claimed to have wanted to read sticking out from the side pocket of his backpack.

Rising from the ground, and tutting when she saw the tear in her skirt and the irreparable scuffs on the toes of her favourite shoes, she nodded her head, "Yes," then instantly regretted it as a wave of dizziness made her brain feel disconnected from the rest of her body.

Albert caught her as she stumbled, darting forward to grab her arms.

"I think perhaps you ought to consider calling an ambulance," he suggested "You may have a concussion."

Jessica sucked in a breath and held it, her eyes focused on the pavement and her head lowered until she felt able to try straightening up again. Her hands were gripping the sleeves of Albert's coat, preventing him from leaving, though that was not a conscious intention.

When she felt able to lift her head, she drew in another deep breath slowly though her nose.

"No, I'm fine," she insisted. "I don't have far to go."

Rex had been watching the exchange with mild interest and was still trying to figure out what was going on.

His human had issued a command to chase the humans, but Rex still questioned who they were and why the old man had wanted him to chase them. Now though, he had figured it out. His first guess on the train had been right – his human did wish to mate with the female. They were touching; something he rarely saw his human do with a female, and they were very close to one another.

Were they going to crack on right now? Rex's eyebrows were doing a dance as he attempted to figure out what his next move should be.

"Um," he nudged the old man's leg with his nose, and when he glanced down, Rex asked, "Should I just take a walk or something? Give you a few minutes?" In his head, Rex was convinced humans did their mating almost exclusively indoors – they were weird like that, but ...

"Just a second, Rex," Albert turned his attention back to Jessica who was letting go of his arms now and looked more or less okay. Concussion wasn't to be taken lightly though and the problems associated with it could manifest long after the initial injury. "How far?" he asked, looking up the street in the direction she had been walking.

Jessica took a step back and stood still to prove she could do so without wobbling. Albert was waiting for an answer, and she could have indicated with her head, but chose instead to say, "It's just around the corner."

"You're sure you don't want to call an ambulance?" Albert had to check.

"No, I'm fine. Really."

She was going to go home and that was the best scenario for Albert, but he knew he couldn't just let her make her own way. If he did, he would spend the rest of the night wondering if she got there without fainting halfway and would forever question if the pair of men who intended ... whatever, would turn up at her house later.

Groaning inside, Albert insisted on walking her home.

Lies

S he really did live just around the corner; the walk to get there taking less than two minutes. They were walking slowly and though she continued to assure Albert that she was fine, and refused to accept his arm or shoulder as an anchor to balance herself, it was clear she was feeling dizzy or off kilter.

Once again fishing the jangling bunch of keys from her bag, Jessica held them up with her left hand so she could sort through them with her right.

Without warning she turned right through a gate toward a large Edwardian terraced house. The front yard was neat and free of weeds and the chequerboard path leading to the front door looked to be an original feature. Though it was worn from age, it was still complete where others they had passed were missing tiles.

"Come in, please," Jessica invited. She had the door open and was paused with one foot inside as she waited for Albert's response.

He had seen her home and now it was time for him to be on his way. He was about to say just that when Rex voiced his opinion.

It wasn't really Rex's fault. He'd been thinking about mating due to his human's behaviour, so when the scent of a female German Shepherd in season wafted out through the open door and into his nostrils, it bypassed his brain and went straight to his paws.

With a bark of excitement, he took off.

Caught completely by surprise, the lead snapped from Albert's hand before he could tighten his grip, and stumbling a pace forward, he got to watch his dog bound past Jessica, down the hallway, and out of sight.

Jessica watched him go, a curious expression on her face, which she showed Albert when she crossed over the threshold and said, "I guess he can smell Delilah."

"Delilah?"

"Nan's dog," Jessica remarked, hanging up her coat and sliding off her shoes. "Please," she beckoned. "The warm air is escaping."

Now with little choice in the matter, Albert dutifully followed Jessica inside and stood to one side so she could close the door.

He had been planning to confirm that she did not live alone - if she wasn't going to call the medical services it was important that there

43

was somebody around to make sure that she was okay – however, he now knew she lived with her grandmother.

Placing his suitcase on the carpet next to Jessica's shoes, Albert slipped off his backpack and his coat, placing all three in a neat pile. He was about to remove his shoes, since he was now in someone's house, when Jessica advised him to stop.

"Please. There's really no need to take them off; the dog doesn't bother to wipe her feet."

Her feet.

It was a girl dog then. The name should have given it away, but one could never be sure. It certainly explained why Rex had shot off with such enthusiasm.

In the pantry beyond the kitchen at the back of the house, Rex had indeed found Delilah, and discovered her to be in a most receptive mood. He could hear his human calling for him, but short of the house catching fire, nothing was going to interrupt his current endeavour.

Albert didn't need to see the dogs to be able to tell what was going on in the pantry, but a quick glance around the door frame confirmed it, nevertheless.

"Righto," he huffed out an impatient breath. "I guess I'm stuck here for a while. I would ask if this was okay, but it's not as if there's anything I can do about it."

Flicking the kettle on and reaching up to take out two mugs from a cupboard, Jessica sniggered.

"Don't worry, gran will be pleased. She was hoping to mate Delilah anyway. She usually uses studs from the kennel club, but your fellow looks like a pedigree,' she observed, sort of asking a question but not framing it as one. Holding up the mugs, she asked, "Is tea all right? I can't offer you anything stronger, I'm afraid. There's no alcohol in the house or gran will drink it."

"Tea will be fine," Albert replied with a nod. "Thank you very much. I really didn't intend to impose."

Facing away from Albert as she busied herself putting tea bags into a teapot, something Albert rarely saw the younger generation doing nowadays, she said, "You are not imposing at all, Albert. I'm not entirely convinced you didn't cause the accident," she lied while fishing a first aid box out from a floor-level cupboard by her feet, "but I am willing to believe your intentions were good and you did stay to make sure I was okay. Those are rare qualities."

It had not escaped Albert that all signs of her wooziness had disappeared the moment her front door closed.

"Could you give me a hand?" she asked, holding up a gauze patch and some tape. "I just want to soak up the blood. I can't do much more without shaving my head and there's no chance that's happening."

Her vanity aside, Albert doubted stitches were necessary. She might have to take care showering or washing her hair for a few days, but the wound was small and would quickly heal.

He helped to apply the sticking tape across her forehead and down over her temple. It was rudimentary, but sufficient for the task.

Checking herself using the camera on her phone, Jessica pouted and frowned before putting the device down and dismissing the head-wound as unimportant.

Fixing Albert in place with her eyes, she said, "So you were reading a story on my newspaper. Care to expand on that? I'm guessing you don't live in Eton."

"Um, no," Albert admitted. "I was on my way to Cornwall, actually."

"Cornwall?" Jessica's eyebrows showed her surprise. "You missed by quite a distance. What on earth could have made you detour so far out of your way?"

Albert chewed on his top lip for a second, taking his time to think carefully about what he wanted to say before deciding it was already too late to play his cards close to his chest - he'd slipped up and given her his real name in the first few seconds of meeting her.

Accepting that his behaviour required some explanation he asked, "Did you read the article about Joseph Lawrence?" It was an opening gambit to see how much background detail he would need to provide.

Jessica's right eyebrow twitched. *How much did the old man know? Who was he? Was it really coincidence that he was in her kitchen now?* She had to wrestle her emotions under control to prevent them from spilling onto her face.

Calmly, she replied. "Yes, I read the article." *Now was not the time to reveal the truth. If he knew more than he was letting on, she would know soon enough.*

Glad he could just explain without having to go over the recent death in her hometown, Albert said, "I'm investigating a series of crimes and what happened to Mr. Lawrence appears to fit the pattern. That is why I altered my intended destination today. I need to be in Cornwall roughly thirty-six hours from now. Ideally tomorrow night, actually, but I can devote tomorrow morning to investigating what happened to him and whether it is indeed what I believe it to be."

"And what is that?" Jessica pinned him, wanting more detail.

The kettle finished getting excited, switching itself off with an audible click that interrupted their conversation. As the noise it had been making fell away, so the sounds coming from the pantry became more noticeable.

Taking two steps to her right, Jessica reached out and closed the pantry door, shutting the dogs' amorous activities behind an inch of solid wood before turning her attention back to the beverages.

Over her shoulder she encouraged, "Please do go on, Albert. I am all ears."

There really wasn't a way around it that he could see. Clearing his throat, he began to explain.

"Joseph worked at the factory that produces Eton Mess puddings for the British market. They sell them in supermarkets and such as I am sure you know. What if I told you that over the last few months there have been people from the food industry mysteriously disappearing all over the country?"

Jessica had poured the hot water into the teapot; she was using teabags though her gran always insisted on loose leaves that went inside a spherical caddy inside the pot. Some leaves always escaped which ruined the experience in her opinion, but gran's opinion would not be shifted.

The pot needed to sit for several minutes now to let the hot water and tea leaves infuse, so she turned back to face Albert and leaned against the counter. She'd heard what he said, but wasn't sure she followed.

"Mysteriously disappearing?"

Albert made a face to acknowledge his words sounded crazy. "Kidnapped, in fact. I was witness to one such event in Biggleswade. It's what set me on this path of investigation as much as anything. It's not just people though. Food and the equipment for making it have been stolen too. Sausage making machinery from a factory in Keswick, Stilton cheese was stolen in Stilton ... the list is a long one and like I said, what happened to Joseph fits the pattern."

Jessica offered a doubtful face.

"He fell to his death if I remember the article correctly."

"The same thing happened to a wine connoisseur in Kent just a few days ago. He was attempting to escape the kidnappers. I am certain of that because half a dozen other people went missing from the same vineyard on the same night, plus hundreds of bottles of wine and a row of mature vines."

"That's hardly conclusive." Jessica wasn't going to be easily convinced.

Her comment caused a wry chuckle to escape Albert's lips.

"That's precisely why you have an old man investigating it all by himself and not a crack team from Scotland Yard. I need to find conclusive proof, to catch them in the act, if I want to convince the police that I am right."

Jessica considered Albert's outlandish tale for a few seconds.

"That's what you came to Eton for," she concluded. "You think these people were after Joseph. Surely though, having failed to get him because he fell and died, they have already left."

Albert sucked in a breath and scratched his head.

"That's a natural conclusion, I'll admit, but that's not what happened in Kent. They missed the man they wanted, so went for the next one in line. They wanted a wine expert, and it didn't matter too much who they got so long as the person knew their stuff. I'm expecting them to default to whoever is the next on their list. The article reported that Mr

Lawrence was a health and safety manager at the firm. I'm not sure why that makes him special, but he must have an immediate successor."

Jessica fell silent, and to hide the expressions crossing her face, turned around to pour the tea.

The old man's tale was fanciful, but she got no indication that he was making it up. If anything, he believed wholeheartedly in what he was saying.

Was it time to come clean? Well, not clean exactly, but to tell Albert just enough to get him to help her? She knew precisely what had happened to Joseph Lawrence and it was nothing to do with food. The old man in her kitchen didn't need to know that though.

She was short on time, undoubtedly in danger, and though she could be fairly sure they had no idea where she was staying – no one did – going to work tomorrow to get the thing she needed was perilous.

Albert, with his outlandish story, was just begging to be unwittingly enrolled to help her.

The Truth, but Still a Lie

Sucking in a deep breath, she picked up the mugs of tea and placed them on the table, then fetched a milk jug from the fridge and a pot containing sugar cubes.

"I need to come clean, Albert," Jessica made herself sound embarrassed. "I work at Wallace's too. I knew Joseph quite well and he was acting strange last week in the build up to what happened."

Albert could not believe his ears.

"You worked with the victim?" Like a lightning bolt striking his brain, the man following Jessica and the attack that nearly happened took on a whole different meaning. Just like Tanya and Baldwin, the man with the flat top and the smaller man he never got a good look at, were agents of the Gastrothief. Just as he thought upon first reading the newspaper story, they were in Eton to grab someone. Joseph fell to his death, and so they switched their aim to target Jessica.

Jessica's voice was quiet and thoughtful when she replied, "I did."

"Then you are in danger." He made the statement before he considered what it might mean. His intervention earlier had been so well timed, that had she not been knocked to the ground, she might never have known anything was occurring. Now, if he convinced her that she had been the target and the Gastrothief's agents would be back, her first action would be to call the police.

He was in a no-win situation.

Changing tack, he sought to confirm, "You didn't see either of the two men?"

Jessica fixed Albert with a level stare. "No. I would have said if I did."

She was being defensive, though Albert chose to let it go without comment as he pressed on.

"One man was very tall – six foot six would be my guess, and he had a flat top haircut, quite a tall one."

"Like *Vanilla Ice*?"

Albert blinked, trying to figure out what her question meant. "I'm not sure what ice cream has to do ..." He stopped mid-sentence when Jessica shoved her phone in his direction.

"He's a rapper from the early nineties," she explained.

The point of course was his hairstyle which was much akin to the one he'd seen on the tall man.

"Yes," Albert replied. "Just like that. Have you seen a tall man with a blonde flat top recently? He would stand out." Albert posed the question very much as if there ought to be no way Jessica wouldn't have spotted him, but not quite so it sounded like an accusation.

Jessica turned away, saying, "Sorry, Albert. I guess I'm not particularly observant."

He pressed on regardless. "The second man was much shorter, with less muscle. Like a boy almost. He couldn't have been much taller than five foot six." Albert considered the description he'd just given, concluding, "That's not even slightly helpful, is it?"

Jessica gave a non-committal shrug.

Another change of tack brought a fresh question. "Why would they target you?" Before Jessica had a chance to answer, Albert added, "They always go after people who are either directly involved in food preparation or have intimate knowledge of recipes." Drawing a blank expression, he tried, "Do you know how to operate the machinery to make an Eton Mess."

Jessica made it clear she was growing bored of the continual questioning, but was polite when she said, "I'm sorry, Albert. You claim they were after me, but I have nothing to do with food at the factory, I'm not a particularly good cook, and there's nothing in my head worth kidnapping me for."

Albert took her response on the chin. It was disappointing, but perhaps she was right. Maybe they wanted her so they could get to someone else. He chose to let it rest. For now.

So it was to his great surprise when Jessica said, "Can you help to keep me safe?"

Stunned by the question, Albert took too long to respond, and Jessica began trying to convince him.

"What if they were after me? You already said the police don't believe you, and that you need to find evidence of this Gastrothief if you want to get them involved. And it's not like I can go to the police myself – what would I even say? I got bumped by a man in the street and there was another man, an older man, who has an outlandish tale about people from the food industry getting kidnapped."

Albert hadn't given it much thought until then but could see her point.

"The police would dismiss me before I even got to the end of the story. If they are who you think they are, then they will be back, right?"

"That's my assumption."

"So you can catch them in the act, right?"

Albert shrugged and made a point of looking down at his ageing body.

"I'm not quite the thieftaker I used to be." At the same time, he was thinking that Rex would do the trick nicely and have the Gastrothief's agents begging for mercy by the time the police arrived. However, another thought forced its way to the front of the queue. "What if they come here to get you? If I'm right about who they are, they are slick and well organised. Some of their colleagues – I haven't seen the two from tonight before – tracked me to my house. It's one of the reasons I need to solve this case: it's not safe for me to go home until I have."

Jessica had been blowing gently onto the surface of her tea, but put the mug down when she answered.

"They won't find me here."

"Why not."

"Because this is not my home."

The surprising statement was followed by a brief explanation: she'd recently caught her boyfriend of two years cheating and had stormed out. He'd only asked her to move in six months earlier. Albert got the sense that the woman could feel her twenties slipping away and was hoping for more than she got. Marriage and children sounded like givens for the average person, yet Albert knew they were goals some never managed to achieve.

Jessica had moved in with her gran less than three days ago, but the way the Gastrothief's agents had come at her from two directions suggested they knew where she was going. There was an answer to that too.

"Martin – that's my ex-boyfriend – lives just down the road. They must have thought I was going there. I hope they do decide to snatch me from his address. He deserves to have someone burst in on him. You know that skanky girl he was cheating with has already moved in?"

Albert had no idea how to respond.

"Sorry," Jessica apologised. "You don't need me burdening you with my silly problems. Listen though, I've just realised I have the perfect cover to get you into the factory tomorrow."

They Really are Crazy

Rex was basking in the glow of post-coital bliss and curled up in the dog bed with Delilah. She had nuzzled into him and was murmuring her thanks and appreciation.

"That's okay, believe me," he replied, staring at the closed door which had been open when he came in. He hadn't heard anyone shutting it, but a simple nudge with his head when they were done and he went looking for water, confirmed it was going to impede his exit.

He felt like going for a run; mating always had that effect on him, and he wanted to eat. Boy did he want to eat. A trip to a public house, as was normal for his human at this time of day, would tick all his boxes. Necessary task complete, he had lost all interest in Delilah and was only with her still because he couldn't get out.

"Do you think they are also mating?" he asked, his eyes glued to the door and his nose working overtime.

Delilah rolled over onto her front and twisted her head so she could look at Rex's face.

"Who are we talking about?"

Rex blinked. "My human and your human."

"Oh, did your human hang around? Normally Edwina sends them off to kill time elsewhere - she doesn't like them in the house. Anyway, Edwina isn't here ..." her voice trailed off as questions formed a queue in her head. "Hold on, if my human isn't here then why are you?"

Rex was getting confused.

"Who is Edwina?"

"My human," Delilah got out of the basket. "She went out more than an hour ago and won't be back for ages. She took Eric with her." Her features carried a warning: Rex needed to start explaining himself or there was going to be trouble. "You're not from the Kennel Club at all, are you?"

Rex twisted his head to the left, trying to understand what she was saying.

"The Kennel Club? Why would I be from the Kennel Club?" To his great surprise, the lady dog who had until moments ago been about as friendly as a lady could get, was now bunching her leg muscles as she prepared to launch herself at him.

Rex couldn't work out what had gone wrong or what he was supposed to do and was given no time to react as she launched herself across the room at his face.

"Oh, I never thought this day would come!" Delilah exclaimed, licking his muzzle all over in her excitement. "So many studs, all with stupidly huge ..." she paused to take a breath, then finished with, "egos," much to Rex's relief. "They were never interested in me. They were only here to ... well, you know. That's what I thought you were. Another stud from the Kennel Club. I cannot express what a relief it is to finally meet a dog who will be my mate for life."

Rex's eyes almost popped from his head.

"I'm sorry, what?"

He got no reply from Delilah who was still busy licking and nuzzling his face and a new question made its way to the fore.

"How many studs are we talking about?"

The door opened and Rex seized the chance to escape.

"I need a drink," he announced, leaping from the bed with such suddenness that Delilah fell forward and found herself licking the wall that Rex had backed into.

Terrified his human might not be there, a wave of relief washed over him when Rex spotted the old man sitting at a table.

"Ready to go?" he asked with an encouraging wag of his tail. "No time to waste, eh? You can almost taste that refreshing beer already, I'll bet. No sense hanging around."

Albert reached down to pat Rex's head. "Happy with yourself, are you, boy?" he asked, completely misinterpreting Rex's excited movements.

"I was," Rex replied, glancing over his shoulder as Delilah left the pantry to join him in the kitchen. Lowering his voice to an urgent whisper, he added, "Now I've got a level five clinger and we need to go." When his human didn't move, he hissed, "You know how they say bitches be crazy? Well, this precise occasion is why. You. Have. To. Get. Me. Out. Of. Here!"

Distracted by what he had just learned from Jessica and going nowhere because there were more questions to ask yet, Albert pointed to Delilah's water bowl.

"Get a drink if you want one, Rex. There's a good fellow. I might even rustle up a couple of gravy bones in a minute."

Following where his human pointed, Rex spotted the water bowl. His mouth *was* dry. Slaking his thirst, his mouth deep into the cool water, he became suddenly aware of another tongue next to his.

Snapping his head up in shock, and with water cascading onto the tiled floor, he stared down at Delilah.

She winked at him. "Come along, lover. We can share a water bowl. I won't bite."

Certain he would be leaving soon, not that soon would be soon enough, Rex cautiously lowered his head again. The moment he started lapping water, Delilah said, "This is nice. Just like an old couple who have been mated for years."

Rex's shocked exclamation of terror resulted in water going up his nose when he breathed in before lifting his head. Snorting, choking, and with cold water attacking the soft membrane of his olfactory system, Rex bucked to get away from the bowl.

Delilah laughed at him. "Aww, so sweet. You'll get used to me though."

Spinning around to face Albert, Rex implored him, "Please tell me we are leaving now."

Rex didn't know whose house they were in, but the scent of another woman, an older one, permeated everything, whereas the smell of the younger lady they'd arrived with was fresh like she had only been staying here a short while. Looking around with concern on his face, Rex wondered why were they not already at a pub getting dinner? And why did Delilah believe he was moving in with her forever?

"We're going to be staying here for the night, Rex," Albert told him while scratching the fur on his head. The news came as quite a shock to Rex.

Behind Rex, Delilah squealed with delight, "Yay!"

Rex blinked and swallowed. "What … what do you mean we're staying here? Why would we be staying here?"

Albert got the sense that Rex was worried about something. His dog's ears were flat; a trait Albert only ever saw when Rex had done something wrong or suspected Albert planned to make him have a bath.

"What's the matter, fella?" he asked, keeping eye contact with his dog.

Delilah came to sit next to Rex, leaning into his side meaningfully.

"We're in love, can't you tell?" Delilah sighed. "Rex is just a bit shell-shocked from the depth of emotion he feels right now."

Rex's eyes were as big as saucers and his heart rate wouldn't calm down, but it was nothing to do with being in love. With Delilah cosying up to him, and his human scratching his ears, he couldn't say what was in his head; Delilah came across as the kind of bitch who would go full postal on him. There was nowhere for him to go.

Or was there?

Bouncing onto all four paws, Rex darted across to the back door. There would be a garden beyond it and a wall or fence he could leap. Escape might seem like an extreme measure, but the situation called for it. His human would be forced to look for him and Rex would lead the old man away, taking him to a public house where they should be, not staying in the den of a psycho hound.

"Okay if I let the dogs out?" Albert called out.

Jessica had gone upstairs to sort out bedding for the spare room and insisted she didn't need any help. She'd also insisted on paying for food and had ordered an Indian feast from a local takeaway. Albert chose to be agreeable. It wasn't what he'd planned for dinner, but saw no reason to turn down her offer.

Besides the fact that she was going to put him directly into a position to catch the Gastrothief's agents in the act, sleeping in Jessica's gran's spare room meant that any slim hope of Chief Inspector Quinn figuring out where Albert was had completely evaporated.

Jessica's voice carried down the stairs, "Sure. There's a switch for the outside light by the door."

The dogs bounded out into the garden, one after the other, Rex pelting hell for leather into the dark only to have his movements thrown into stark relief when Albert found the light switch.

Skidding to a halt, Rex looked around in mute horror.

The garden was a dead end. Six-foot wooden fence panels peeked out from behind fifteen-foot tall leylandii trees and other tall plants that went all the way down both sides of the garden and across the bottom edge.

Delilah came to stand in front of Rex's face, a question on her brow.

"Is there something the matter, Rex?"

"Err, oh, um, no. No, of course not. Why would you think that?" *Dear Lord there has to be a way out of here!*

"Oh, good," Delilah brightened. "For a moment there I thought you were going to leave me like all the other dogs always do."

Unable to find a way out of the garden that did not involve trying to run through a fence panel, Rex sighed forlornly and traipsed back to the house.

Melissa Medina

While the dogs were outside and he was waiting for Jessica to return, Albert took out his phone.

"Battery's almost dead again," he remarked to himself. Looking around he spotted a charger plugged in to a socket behind the kitchen counter. He waited until Jessica appeared from upstairs before asking, "Mind if I plug this in?"

"No. Go ahead."

The battery icon flashed into life to show it was charging and he turned his attention toward his host as she went over her plan in a little more detail.

"There's an Eton Mess making competition for charity tomorrow. It's an annual thing," she revealed. "Have you ever made an Eton Mess?"

Albert grimaced. His skill in the kitchen was most notable for its lack of existence.

"I have not," he admitted, adding, "I'm a fast learner though," because he didn't want to put Jessica off now that she was offering to help. "Is it a big affair, this competition?"

Jessica skewed her lips to one side as she thought about her answer.

"Sort of. I guess. The local press will be there, and they get a bunch of spectators and visitors because it's a factory open day too. There will be tours, which plays nicely into our hands, and stalls where other vendors will be selling their wares."

"Is it likely we will be able to enter at such short notice?" Albert didn't want to get his hopes up.

Jessica chuckled, "I'm more or less running the event. Don't worry."

Albert accepted her response without comment because his brain had moved on already. That the timing of the Gastrothief agents' visit coincided with the competition could not be coincidence, and realising that led to another question he voiced before Jessica could answer the first. "Why would they have targeted Joseph? They always go after people who are either experts in making the dish or those who can operate the machinery. Is he either one of those?" Albert doubted Joseph fell into the first category and as the health and safety manager was surely too far removed from the manufacturing process to know it intimately.

Jessica's reply removed any ambiguity, "He won the Eton Mess competition about seven times in the last twenty years. That includes last year."

Albert shook his head and remembered the headline in the newspaper: it said the victim was an Eton Mess Champion.

He was right. He was right about everything and all he'd needed was a headline in a newspaper to steer him here. Maybe he didn't need to go to Cornwall at all. If he could catch them in the act tomorrow, his need to stay under the radar and on the run from the authorities would be over.

Oh, it would still take some explaining, and most likely a bunch of hours stuck in an interview room while they grilled him twelve ways to Sunday. Nevertheless, if he caught the Gastrothief's agents, he would be able to call his children and they would see to it the truth was swiftly exposed. He couldn't do that yet though for he was certain their phones were being monitored. They had helped him and were currently suffering a period of suspension while their father's possible involvement in acts of terrorism was investigated.

"He was a recognised expert in making an Eton Mess," Albert remarked. "You say a local paper covers the event?"

"Every year."

Albert gave himself a few seconds to think about being in such close proximity to a newspaper journalist. It was only a local newspaper and he thought it likely that there would only be one person there probably doubling up as the photographer and reporter in one. Whoever it was, Albert figured they would not be too hard to avoid at the event. It wasn't ideal, but this was probably the best shot he was going to get. Not least because he'd seen what he believed to be the Gastrothief's agents this evening and he'd not seen either of them before. Hopefully that meant they wouldn't recognise him.

Albert still thought it entirely possible that it was going to be Tanya with a new partner in Cornwall. Previously he'd only seen her with a man called Baldwin; the man whose phone he now had in his possession. But Baldwin was too badly injured following a fight with Rex for him to show up with Tanya twenty-four hours from now.

What Albert did not know was that Baldwin was never going to show up anywhere ever again. Taking advantage of her partner's injuries, Tanya had chosen to kill him. His body now rested in a shallow grave not far from the M25 motorway.

Accepting that he was going to do whatever it took, Albert asked, "You said that Joseph won the competition several times. Is there anyone else who has won it multiple times?"

Jessica did not need to think about her response. "Oh, yes. A local lady ..." she paused, her eyes staring into the distance with an expression that made Albert believe she was attempting to dredge her memory for a name. Jessica's features shifted with the arrival of an annoyed face as she snatched up her phone. Flying fingers danced across the screen, but it only took her a few seconds to find the information she wanted. "Melissa Medina. I knew it was something like that. Where was I? Oh, yes. Mrs Medina has won the competition almost as many times as Joseph and caused quite a stink last year when she accused the judges of bias. She felt that anyone working at the factory ought to be disqualified from entry and was quite vocal about it."

Her opinion was just background trivia so far as Albert was concerned. He was more interested in identifying a potential secondary target for the Gastrothief's agents. Much like with the wine connoisseur in Kent, when they failed to obtain the person they wanted, they deferred to a secondary target. Mrs Medina was now the probable target in Eton.

He had no way to be sure, yet Albert felt certain they would strike as soon as they were able. Would they already know the name of their secondary target? Albert thought it highly probable and asked, "I don't suppose you have any idea where Mrs Medina lives, do you?"

The question clearly surprised Jessica and of course she had no idea where it was that the lady lived, only that she was local. She knew that because in her ranting at the judges last year when she was awarded second place, her status as a citizen of Eton was one of her strongest points - Joseph Lawrence did not live in the local area, Albert discovered.

Jessica's response came across as dismissive, like there was nothing to worry about. However, Albert wasn't about to let it go.

"Their best strategy is to move on her tonight. I'm not suggesting anyone else will make the connection, but if we fail to act and they take her, any chance to catch them tomorrow will be gone."

Jessica stifled a sigh. "So what are you saying?"

"That we must warn her. I need a phone number or an address. If she is local, we can go there."

Jessica had to bite down her first response. Albert came across as a sweet old man, but this thing with the Gastrothief was nuts. Contacting Mrs Medina was a complete waste of time, except that she needed to keep Albert on her side if she was to use him tomorrow. Accepting her fate, Jessica grabbed her phone and used it to search for a phone number. A phone call she could tolerate, but she wasn't going out again.

Thankfully, Melissa Medina was listed, so she offered Albert her phone – she wasn't going to be the one to make what would sound like a crank call.

Albert pressed the green button and waited for the call to connect, running through what he would say in his head.

"Hello," a woman's voice answered. To Albert's ears she sounded in her late fifties.

"Good evening. My name is Albert Smith, I'm hoping to speak with Melissa Medina. It's to do with the Eton Mess contest tomorrow."

"Speaking."

Her reply was terse, her tone somewhere between impatient and annoyed.

Albert pressed on, "Mrs Medina, I am a private investigator and have reason to believe there may be persons willing to target you …"

"What? What is this nonsense? What did you say your name was?"

"Albert Smith." Albert attempted to continue but was cut off again.

"Are you competing too? Is that what this is?"

"Um."

"You are, aren't you! I bet you work for Wallace's too! Of all the dirty tactics ... phoning me at home the night before the contest to try to scare me off. Well, that just proves how dangerous you all believe I am. I'm going to win, d'you hear? I'm going to win and there's nothing you can do to stop me!"

"Please, Mrs Medina, I need to warn you. Your success in recent years could make you a target."

"No! You need to listen to my warning, Albert Smith. If I for one second believe anyone at Wallace's is attempting to interfere with my puddings tomorrow, I will scream to high heaven and the judges will jolly well listen this time. I'll not be cheated two years running!"

The sound of the phone being slammed down echoed in Albert's ear.

"That didn't go too well, did it?" Jessica remarked.

Albert kept his mouth shut and handed back the phone.

He'd tried, he really had. Part of him wanted to get Melissa's address and try to talk sense into her face to face, but he couldn't see how he was going to have any better success that way. In fact, he thought it more likely she would call the police if he turned up at her house.

And so his plan was set. Albert was going to enter the Eton Mess competition in the morning. There was a definite space for him to do so because Joseph's place was now free. Jessica assured him that she could deal with the particulars in the morning. Her position at the firm, that of executive assistant to the CEO, ensured that she had all the necessary contacts at her disposal.

To prove her point, she emailed the event organiser.

A whining noise at the back door brought Albert's head and eyes around to look in its direction. It sounded like Rex, which was odd. More commonly, when he is shut in the garden and wants to be let back into the house, he barks. Loudly.

Indicating his intention with his eyes as he got up, Albert got a nod of approval from Jessica, and opened the back door. He did this with too little caution and was rewarded with the door slamming into both shinbones as his dog barged through the gap before it was wide enough to accommodate his shoulders.

Swearing under his breath, and glaring at his dog, Albert bent over to rub his legs.

"In a hurry tonight are we, boy?"

"He's just excited," murmured Delilah, sauntering through the door behind Rex.

Rex was thinking that his current state of mind was more akin to panicked than excited. Terrified might be another good word.

The doorbell rang, both dogs snapping out a bark automatically. The suddenness of it made Jessica jump.

Putting a hand to her chest as if to calm her heart, she said, "That will be our takeaway arriving, I should imagine." Striding across the room to follow the dogs who had both belted in the direction of the front door, she swapped her phone for her purse without breaking stride.

Reaching for the wallet in his back pocket, Albert gave chase.

"You must let me pay, dear. You are offering to put me up, after all."

"We'll split it," Jessica offered, gripping Rex by his collar so she could haul him back a few feet. Passing him to Albert, she then did the same with Delilah, and only once Albert had both dogs under control, did she deem it safe to open the door.

Back in the kitchen moments later, the house was filling with glorious smells. They were emanating from the brown paper bag placed in the centre of the kitchen table. Jessica was busy fetching crockery and cutlery and had instructed Albert to root around in the fridge for a cold beverage if he wanted one.

Albert selected a supermarket brand can of soda, fetching one for Jessica too at her request.

He was hungry, there was no denying it, and now that the Indian food was here, the scent of it was making his stomach rumble.

Hearing it, Jessica remarked, "Goodness. When did you last eat?"

Albert grinned as he settled into one of the kitchen table chairs.

"It's been a few hours."

He was looking forward to tucking in, but before he got the chance, the sound of someone coming through the front door filled his body with adrenaline.

Daddy!

Albert shot his eyes at Jessica, the question in them requiring no vocalisation. To his surprise, she chuckled.

The wobbly voice of an elderly lady echoed into the kitchen from the entrance hall. "Ooh, that smells good."

Jessica raised her voice. "Hi, Gran. Did you win?" To Albert's confused face, she said, "Gran goes to bingo with her friends on a Saturday night."

Sitting obediently by his human's feet, Rex's muscles had tensed when he heard the front door opening, but he had not suffered the same flash of worry that gripped Albert. Rex's nose told him that it was an elderly person entering the abode, and her scent matched up to one that permeated everything in the house.

However, the elderly lady wasn't the only thing Rex could smell entering the house, and it was the second being accompanying the human that sent a spike of panic through his heart.

He stayed put, getting some small comfort in his strange and unnerving surroundings from being close to Albert. Delilah dashed out to greet the new arrivals and Rex could hear her saying something in the entrance hall though he could not make out the words.

"Dig in," Jessica encouraged, rising from her chair to leave the room. "I've just realised I forgot to tell gran she has an additional guest."

Rex watched the door, his heart banging in this chest. Delilah had mentioned Eric earlier, but at the time Rex's mind had been elsewhere, drifting along in a fog of recently released endorphins, and he had ignored it.

Now, he felt certain he knew precisely who Eric was, and a moment later a four-month-old German Shepherd puppy careened through the kitchen door.

"Daddy!" the over-excited pup cried the moment he clapped eyes on Rex.

"What!"

"Daddy!"

"What? No. No, no, no, no, no."

The pup bounded across the room, colliding with Albert's chair just as the old man was starting to rise.

Launching himself at Rex's face, Eric cheered, "Daddy! Mum said you would come back one day. She promised me and here you are!"

Delilah followed behind Eric at a slow walking pace.

Rex's hit her with panic-stricken eyes that had no impact on her contended expression.

"Oh, look at the two of you. So perfect together," she remarked with a happy sigh.

Albert, now on his feet, reached down to pat the meaty part of Rex's neck.

"Looks like you've got a ready-made family there, boy."

Delilah sighed again. "I couldn't have put it better myself."

While his dog descended into a nightmarish scenario from which he could currently see no escape, Albert was doing his best to apologise for what once again felt like an intrusion.

"I've no wish to impose," he called out to the unseen homeowner. "I have a room reserved at the Dog and Duck."

"The Dog and Duck?" repeated the lady of the house as she strolled into the kitchen. "That place is a dump. No one should have to stay there."

"Gran this is Albert ..." Jessica began to explain.

"Here, what happened to your head?" asked Jessica's gran.

"I, err. I fell." Flapping a dismissive hand, Jessica said, "Albert came to my aid, gran. He's new in town and I offered him the spare room. I hope that's ok. It's just for a couple of nights."

"Probably just the one night," Albert corrected Jessica's statement. He was on his feet now and moving to introduce himself as decorum dictated. He couldn't yet see who he was addressing; her form was obscured in its entirety by Jessica.

Realising she was in the way, Jessica moved to the side, and Albert stuck out his hand.

"Albert Smith. Thank you for your hospitality. I really don't mean to impose though. Please send me on my way if stopping for the night is in any way inconvenient." He didn't want to move on, crashing for one night was safe, cheap, and easy as he was already here, but even if the Dog and Duck turned out to be a dump as Jessica's gran claimed, it would serve his purposes for the night, and he doubted the police had any idea where he was or how to find him.

Jessica's gran was a shade under five feet tall and slender like her granddaughter. Though age had robbed her skin of the elasticity it once possessed, she was still attractive. Guessing her age to be something north of eighty, Albert was pleased to feel steel in her grip when she took his hand.

"Ooh, you're a big one," she remarked, keeping hold of Albert's hand. "Are you single?"

Jessica gasped, "Gran!"

"What? I'm not getting any younger, you know. Every chance could be my last chance."

To Albert, the refuge of an unknown address no longer seemed as enticing as it had. Looking down at his hand where Jessica's gran still held it and back up into her twinkling, mischievous eyes, he questioned what an appropriate response might be. His list of options ranged from, 'Sorry, I was recently widowed' to 'I'm a bit old for all that' and all the way to 'Get away from me, you mad old cow!'

He was saved from the need to pick one of them when Jessica's gran screeched with laughter and finally set his hand free.

"I do like it when they get all nervous. I'm Edwina Blackwood," she finally gave Albert her name. "Please stay for as long as you need, Albert. It's no imposition at all." Shifting her eyes so she was addressing Jessica, Edwina asked, "Have you shown him his room yet?"

Jessica was settling into her chair and beginning to open cartons of Indian food.

"No, Gran, we haven't been here long enough to get to that yet."

"Well put him in the spare room at the back of the house." Edwina replied, pausing to wink at Albert before she added, "That one doesn't have a lock on the door."

From the corner into which he found himself backed, Rex provided his thoughts on the matter, "Not so funny now is it?"

The Bad Guy

"S he. Got. Away." The words were spoken slowly and deliberately by a man sitting in a hot tub. Smoke from a fat cigar lodged between the index and middle fingers of his right hand drifted lazily into the night sky. The backdrop to his outdoor hot tub was a lake and beyond that an exclusive golf club to which he was a member. The membership alone cost more than most lawyers made in a year.

Facing him, not that he was bothering to make eye contact, were Chrissy and Kasper, at their employer's lakeside house to report on their evening's lack of success.

"It happens," Chrissy explained, her voice deliberately neutral. Her employer, a top money launderer for various organised crime families, had a fiery temper and was known for violent reprisals against those who displeased him. "We had her cornered, but just as Kasper was about to take her, an old man intervened."

"An old man?" Again, he spoke the words slowly, and with an unmistakable edge – if he didn't hear something he liked soon there would be consequences. Chrissy was cute even if she did tend to dress like a boy most of the time, and she was efficient, but that didn't mean he couldn't replace her. Perhaps though, it might be better to kill her giant ox of a lackey, Kasper. It would focus her attention or confirm she wasn't the operative he thought she was.

"Yes, Mr Crumley," Chrissy looked pained as she attempted to explain. "I believe it was nothing more than bad luck on our part. The old man had a large dog with him." She chose to leave out the part about the old man setting the dog on Kasper. He clearly read the situation for what it was, but telling her employer about it would only result in more questions. "I believe the dog got loose," she lied, "but the point is there would have been a witness and it wasn't possible for us to grab the old man as well without the dog alerting the entire neighbourhood."

Chrissy was not concerned that Kasper might comment and ruin her lie, he knew well enough to keep his mouth shut. She was the one who did the talking and that had always been the rule. He was not paid to think.

Continuing, since Mr Crumley hadn't spoken, she added, "Jessica Fletcher clearly doesn't have the information that Joseph took, or she would have already acted upon it. We will get her in the morning before she gets to work."

Percy Crumley took a long draw on his cigar, holding the smoke for a few seconds before exhaling a large cloud. All the while his eyes were locked on a point across the lake. However, to ensure his next point was received with absolute clarity, he twisted his body around to lock eyes with the diminutive blonde woman.

"I'm not paying you to guess. She attempted to access the exact same files as Joseph Lawrence. He downloaded the files and saved them onto a portable memory device. That woman, Jessica Fletcher, is either in possession of that device or knows enough to go snooping for the information herself. Somehow the two of them obtained the access code from that greedy idiot Walsh and have only been caught because I have additional, and unbeatable security precautions in place. Regardless of my security, were they not so foolish as to login using their own credentials, we would have no idea who they are."

Percy Crumley stared into Chrissy's eyes. "I gave you a very simple job. Collect her and bring her to me. Do you have any idea what would happen to me if the police seized the money in those accounts?"

Chrissy swallowed, nerves getting the better of her. The question was rhetorical, she felt certain, and she chose not to answer.

Instead, she repeated, "We will get her in the morning before she gets to work."

"Why are you not getting her now? You have her address do you not?"

A grimace flickered across Chrissie's face. "She isn't staying there, Mr Crumley."

Her announcement led to more questions because her employer knew the plan was to intercept Jessica on her way home. Mr Crumley would have 'questioned' her to be certain she hadn't shared the information with anyone else, and then she would have mysteriously disappeared.

Dismissing his hired assassins with a final warning to get it right or pick a grave, Percy Crumley went back to watching the lake.

FULL English

Albert awoke to the delicious scent of bacon cooking. Momentarily confused, as he often was upon waking in a new place, it took him a moment to recall where he was and why he was there. Edwina's spare room was pleasantly decorated as a guest bedroom and the bed on which he had slept was comfortable if a little spongy.

Sleep had been fitful, concern that Edwina might think it a good idea to visit him in the night, not only keeping him awake initially, but causing him to wake each time he heard a noise from within the house.

Mercifully, she didn't.

Without a bathroom of his own and worried he might bump into Edwina in a state of undress, Albert chose to dress himself before leaving the room. His fears were for naught for he found the upstairs of the house to be abandoned.

For the first time in more than a year, Rex wasn't with him. Delilah's puppy, Eric, made so much noise when Rex attempted to follow Albert upstairs, they left all three dogs sleeping together in a pile in the pantry. Albert thought Rex would be happy with that arrangement, yet it was clear from his dog's face when he bade him goodnight that he would rather be anywhere else.

Heading downstairs just a few minutes later with clean teeth and a shaved face, Albert's plan was to take Rex for a walk.

"You've just missed them," advised Edwina when Albert found her in the kitchen. "Jessica took all three of them to the park just a few minutes ago." The homeowner shot Albert a quick glance over her left shoulder before turning her attention back to the cooker.

There were three pans with flames burning away beneath them, and Albert could hear the fan whirring inside the oven.

"Do you think I should go after them?" Albert asked. "I should imagine three dogs could be quite a handful."

Edwina was slow to answer. Preoccupied with what her hands were doing, she opened the oven to remove a large Pyrex dish into which she up ended a pan of sausages.

Albert's stomach rumbled hungrily.

Bumping the oven door closed once more with a hip, Edwina dropped the frying pan into a bubble-filled sink, and finally turned to face her guest.

"No need," she replied with a smile. "They'll be back soon enough. Besides, I'm about ready to serve breakfast and we wouldn't want it to ruin now, would we?"

Accepting his fate, for it was not a terrible one, Albert settled into a dining chair where Edwina indicated.

"Toast or fried bread?" she asked.

"Toast, please."

"Eggs scrambled, fried, boiled, or poached?"

"Fried, please."

The questions continued, Edwina working through more options than Albert would have expected in a high-class hotel. She had gone to some effort, that much was clear, and while Albert felt a natural urge to assure her it was not necessary, he also suspected the lady of the house was rather enjoying having someone to cater for.

To make conversation while he waited Albert asked, "Was Eric the only pup in the litter?"

Edwina cackled in a way that was becoming familiar.

"Goodness, no. I breed Delilah once a year, so she shouldn't have been messing around with Rex, truth be told." Edwina chose that moment to turn about so she could hit her guest with mischievous eyes. "But hormones are hormones," she remarked, meaningfully. "Eric is just the last pup and I'm not sure what to do with him."

"Oh? Is there a problem?"

"Did you not see his tail?" Edwina asked. Seeing the blank expression on Albert's face, she supplied, "He's missing the last third or so. He's no good to a breeder. I could still sell him, but I wouldn't get much. Selling pedigree pups once a year makes me enough money to have a few luxuries."

Albert ran out of things to say and was trying to think of a new line of conversation when Edwina announced his breakfast was ready.

Staring down at the plate placed before him, Albert marvelled at a sumptuous feast stacked far higher than he would ever expect to see at a restaurant. Not only that, it served as a demonstration that Edwina was adept in the kitchen.

Gripping his knife and fork as if they were weapons with which he intended to vanquish his first meal of the day, Albert stared down at his burgeoning plate and wondered where to start.

"Jessica tells me you're entering the Eton Mess competition today," remarked Edwina as she settled into the chair opposite Albert's. It was a conversation starter that required a response.

"Um, yes," Albert mumbled, noting that his host had served herself only a single slice of toast. "That is the plan." He wondered how much Jessica had told her grandmother. Did she know about the Gastrothief?

Their eyes met, and Albert froze, wondering what she was going to say next.

Edwina swallowed the piece of toast she had been chewing and smiled across the table.

"Tuck in, tuck in," she encouraged. "You'll want a full belly before you tackle the day."

Albert ducked his eyes to take in his plate of breakfast once more. It really was a FULL English this time.

Popping a slice of yolk covered sausage into his mouth, he almost choked when Edwina continued, "And they do say the way to a man's heart is through his stomach."

Coughing and spluttering, he was denied the opportunity to respond by Jessica's return. The sound of the front door opening was immediately followed by a stampede of canine feet on the hallway carpet.

Rex was first to arrive.

"Old man you have got to get me out of here!" he whined at Albert, his face right up against his human's arm.

Misinterpreting what his dog was trying to tell him, Albert pushed Rex away. "No begging at the table, Rex." That he planned to feed Rex a worthwhile portion of his breakfast the moment his host wasn't watching could not be voiced aloud.

Shunted back a yard by his human, Rex stared forlornly at the old man's face, imploring him to understand the gravity of his current situation.

Across the room, Eric, was lapping noisily from the water bowl. At four months, the puppy was one quarter the size he would be when fully grown. His fur was still the puppy fuzz he'd been born with, and his latest growth spurt had added inches to his legs to make him gangly. At the park, Rex had watched as Eric bounded around in a perpetually excited manner, his limbs barely under control like a giraffe on roller-skates.

Having a puppy as a companion was not a problem per se, but Eric's insistence on telling all the other dogs in the park that his daddy had finally returned was giving Rex a twitch.

Delilah sidled up next to him.

"Everything all right, lover?"

"Oh, sure, yes," Rex gabbled. "But ..."

"Yes?"

"Well, I'm not actually Eric's father, am I," he pointed out.

Delilah nuzzled in closer to him, whispering things in Rex's ear that made his tail stiffen. When she pulled away, she bit his ear playfully, and murmured, "He needs a father figure, and I have everything you could want, wouldn't you agree?"

Rex was finding it rather difficult to concentrate. There was something going on between his back legs, and there didn't seem to be enough blood left in his head to think straight.

"But what will you tell him when I leave?" he managed to mumble.

"Leave? What makes you think you're leaving? Your human appears to be quite at home."

It was true, he did. Rex watched his human tuck into a large plate of breakfast - a steady source of food would be enough to make Rex want to stay in one place. Was it any different for the old man?

Genuinely concerned he was going to find himself stuck with Delilah and Eric, Rex couldn't figure out what his next move should be. Did he tell her how he felt - that he was happy being a bachelor dog, and risk her wrath? Or was he better off keeping quiet to see how things played out?

Delilah wandered away before Rex could reach a decision, and he let go a breath he didn't realise he'd been holding. Sagging a little, he began to lower himself to the floor only to stop halfway when Albert hissed at him.

Edwina had finished her toast and removed herself to deal with the pots and pans in the kitchen sink. Jessica was loading more bread into the toaster and had a sausage clamped delicately between index finger and thumb. She asked her Gran a question before taking a bite and reaching into the refrigerator to take out the butter.

Now that no one was watching, Albert grasped the opportunity to off load a portion of his cripplingly huge breakfast.

"Here, boy. Help an old man out, won't you?"

Albert carefully offered the items without taking his eyes off the two ladies by the kitchen sink. He knew only too well that Rex would take them and was more worried about getting caught.

Rex snaffled two sausages, a slice of bacon, and two pieces of grilled tomato, swallowing each of them without bothering to chew. When another piece of bacon appeared, so too did Eric.

"Oooh, bacon!" the pup squealed excitedly.

Fearing he might be denied his prize, Rex lunged.

"Arrrrrggghhhh!"

Albert snatched his hand out of Rex's mouth, bringing his fingers up to eye level to confirm they were all still there.

"Something the matter?" asked Edwina.

Both ladies were now looking Albert's way, their eyebrows hiked in question.

Forcing a smile onto his face, Albert collected his knife from the table, and despite his throbbing digits, said, "I bit my tongue. That's all. It caught me by surprise."

The frowns on their faces made it clear the ladies thought his reaction was a little extreme, but they returned to what they were doing which gave Albert a chance to scowl downwards at his dog only to find that Rex was no longer there.

Missing Something

His offers to help with the washing up were turned down; Edwina insisting that no man would ever do chores in her house. It came across as yet another example of the widow going out of her way to make herself appealing.

Albert couldn't figure out how to respond, so took himself back upstairs to pack his things and get ready for the day. He'd managed a quick whispered conversation with Jessica in the hallway – they were leaving soon to get to the factory. She seemed unnaturally keen to help Albert confirm Joseph's death was at the hands of the Gastrothief's agents.

In his opinion, any normal person would want nothing to do with it, but this wasn't the first time in recent months that he'd found a companion willing to give assistance.

His entry to the competition was already confirmed, Jessica emailing the organisers again this morning to confirm there was a position open following Joseph's unexpected and tragic 'accident'.

All they had to do was get there.

"Won't I need equipment and ingredients?" Albert had asked.

Jessica nodded. "Yes. Gran said we can take what we need from her cupboards and there's a supermarket on the way where we can grab some fresh strawberries, cream, and the other things you'll need. You have to make four puddings; the judges mark the entrants on consistency of presentation too."

Folding his pyjamas to pack them away, Albert thought about the likelihood of looking like a fool when he demonstrated how incapable he was of making something as simple as a pudding. The strawberries he could probably manage to hull and slice, the cream he might even be able to whip. Making a meringue though? Not a chance. He knew it was something to do with eggs, but thereafter his knowledge died.

It really didn't matter, obviously. He was going there to see if he could catch the Gastrothief's agents, not win a contest. He'd seen them last night and didn't think they had gotten a good enough look at him for them to recognise him today.

Placing his suitcase on the carpet and picking up his backpack – he would need it today for Rex's things – he told himself to think positively and set out to head downstairs.

Jessica was taking the dogs into the factory with her. She needed to be there today even though it was a Sunday. According to her, more than half the staff would be in work – it was part of their contract and the hours they worked today would be paid at double time. The open day, the factory tours, and all that went with it, demanded she was there, but she would be in her office for the most part and often took Delilah with her.

He'd asked about her head wound only to be assured it was nothing to be concerned about. Her hair was styled a little differently today and it hid the site of the small wound.

"Ready?" Jessica asked when Albert was halfway down the stairs. She was coming out of the kitchen with the three dogs following her.

Albert nodded that he was. "Is it all right if I leave my suitcase here? Hopefully, we'll get lucky and the people I am looking for will present themselves sooner rather than later." He didn't add that if they failed to show, he was going to have to decide whether to hang around or push on to Cornwall. Tanya and Baldwin were due to be there tonight, but had that plan changed? Would they send someone else? Would they put it off for a month? He had no way of knowing and the uncertainty meant that staying here where he felt certain the Gastrothief had operatives was the sensible thing to do.

Edwina shuffled out of the kitchen behind her granddaughter.

"Of course, Albert," she replied on Jessica's behalf, a twinkle in her eye again. "Would you like me to put your clothes through the laundry? I can have them cleaned and ironed by the time you get back." Albert was about to thank her but kindly refuse her offer when she added, "Or I can hang them in my wardrobe if you prefer."

"Gran!" sighed Jessica.

Albert choked on what he had been about to say, his eyes bugging from his head.

"Um, sorry, I need to travel to Cornwall tonight." Even if he wasn't successful today and chose to hang around, he wasn't staying another night in the house of a maneater.

"Ooh, Cornwall," grinned Edwina. "That sounds lovely. And romantic," she tagged on the end of her sentence, acting as if Albert had straight out invited her to elope with him.

Albert was all but running when his feet hit the pavement outside.

Jessica was laughing at him.

"You'll have to forgive gran."

"Will I?" Albert questioned.

"She's just lonely. Granddad died thirty years ago. She's lived alone ever since."

"Well, I'm not looking to replace him."

"I don't think that is what gran has in mind."

"No, I know what she has in mind," Albert muttered.

His comment made Jessica laugh again. "She's probably just teasing."

Albert chose not to reply. He wasn't so sure Edwina had been teasing at all. Though he had no experience from which to draw, he'd heard many stories about retirement homes and how the residents in them acted like horny teenagers. Perhaps it was knowing they had limited years left to live, or maybe it was wishing they'd done more of it when they were younger. Whatever the case, Edwina was displaying the exact same behaviour and it was making Albert more than a little uncomfortable.

It was a short walk – less than a mile – to the factory, which suited Albert. It was a nice day, and he enjoyed the fresh air.

As planned, they stopped at a supermarket for the ingredients they needed, Albert selecting the items Jessica listed and paying for them at the till. They wouldn't all fit in his backpack, though most of them did, so the lighter items went into a carrier bag.

"Here, let me carry that," Jessica held out a hand to take the bag.

Albert cocked an eyebrow. He knew it was no longer cool to be chivalrous – many now considered opening a door for a lady to be an act of chauvinism, yet he wasn't about to let Jessica carry his shopping.

"I've got it," he replied, hoping she would let it go at that.

She didn't.

"You're carrying everything already, Albert. Carrying one shopping bag seems the least I can do given how you have so generously offered to help me today."

Albert's feet stopped moving, his eyebrows dancing while his brain dissected Jessica's sentence. He hadn't heard it wrong.

"Helping you? How am I helping you? You're the one who is helping me to catch the Gastrothief. Aren't you?" he asked, confused.

Jessica's cheeks coloured and she snagged the shopping bag from his hand to cover her embarrassment.

"Yes, of course. What I meant was that you are going out of your way to catch the people who hurt Joseph. He was such a nice man. I didn't believe it was suicide or accidental death."

She hurried toward the exit, leaving Albert to frown. The notion that he was missing something had surfaced. It was a familiar feeling, an old companion if you will. The man with the flat top hair cut had been following Jessica last night. She assured Albert it couldn't be anything to do with the food; she wasn't a competition winner and had nothing to do with the food being made. He couldn't explain why they had chosen to target her, but he knew he hadn't imagined it.

So what was he missing?

Watching her through the shop's glass front, he saw Jessica gather the dogs from the tether point and set off to catch up with her. Whether it was something or nothing, he was going to have to figure it out, but it couldn't take priority over catching the Gastrothief's agents.

Back on the pavement outside, Albert could see the factory ahead of them. What he didn't see was the two people from last night. They were in a different car, the previous one reduced to a cube a fraction of the car's former size.

They needed to snatch the girl and would take the old man too without giving it a second thought. The dogs though, three now, not just one, were a problem. Jessica Fletcher was heading to work, that much they knew in advance, and they were going to have to try to get her there.

In Dogged Pursuit

While Albert was passing through the gates of the factory, several counties away, Chief Inspector Quinn was passing through an altogether different portal: the front door of Roy and Beverly Hope's house.

"He's not here, old boy," Roy aimed his remark at the unwelcome police officer even as his wife invited him in and offered their guest a cup of tea. "And if I knew where he was, I would most certainly not tell you."

Roy's right arm was in a sling, the result of an errant bullet carving a path through the edge of his shoulder. The wound was only two days' old and painful enough that it woke him each time he turned over in the night.

Chief Inspector Quinn had doffed his hat and was using a mirror by the front door to straighten his hair.

"Yes, Mr Hope ..."

"Wing Commander," Roy insisted.

Ian Quinn gave a curt nod of acknowledgement and started again. He wasn't enthralled about addressing the old man so formerly, but rank played a big part in his life, and he understood the desire to retain it after retirement.

"Wing Commander," he started again. "Aiding and abetting Albert Smith will only prolong the time he is on the run. Your friend is no spring chicken. I dare say being pursued by the police will do his health no good at all."

Roy scowled at his guest.

"You underestimate him, Sir. Albert Smith is not only far wilier than you think, he is also right."

"Right?" Quinn's right eyebrow encouraged clarity.

A small snort escaped Roy's nose.

"Sugar, dear?" Beverly asked, calling from the kitchen where the kettle was beginning to get noisy.

The two men were still standing in the hall leading from the front door.

"Yes. He's right," Roy narrowed his eyes at the chief inspector. "The Gastrothief is real. The people Albert is being forced to chase all by himself are real. Your attention should be focussed on helping him, not trying to stop him."

Sensing an opening, Quinn changed tactic.

"And help him is precisely what I want to do. If there is someone else behind the explosion in Whitstable, I need to know who it is. Two nights ago, Leon Harold reported two people entered his house. If we accept that Albert has in fact uncovered something, then for his own safety, as much as anything else, he needs to surrender himself so the professionals can take over. I only want to help him."

"Is that why all three of his children have been suspended pending an enquiry?" Roy shot back. He didn't know Chief Inspector Quinn at all and knew that Albert didn't either. But he'd heard Albert's daughter, Selina, talking about him, and the man came across as a person focussed solely on advancing his career.

Leon Harold's statement made it impossible for the police to believe that Albert was behind the events at the wine connoisseur's house, but equally, no one believed that the Gastrothief was real. There was no evidence, nothing to suggest Albert's theory was anything other than a fanciful tale dreamed up by an old man. Yes, he'd seen something, but to claim there was a James Bond style supervillain behind it ... well, it was met with the ridicule it deserved.

What Roy didn't know was that Ian Quinn was hoping Albert Smith *was* onto something. He didn't for one moment believe in the Gastrothief, but the old detective had successfully identified the likelihood of explosives in Whitstable and had then tracked a couple to a house near Rochester airport where he'd prevented a kidnapping.

If he could find Albert Smith, interrogate him until he knew what the old man knew, and then use it to make the bust himself ... well, that was how promotions were gained. Besides, he couldn't very well openly admit he'd refused to take Albert Smith seriously about the explosives. It would be a black mark against his name, and he'd spent years making sure any mistakes he made landed firmly on someone else's plate.

No, Albert Smith was going to be arrested and then Chief Inspector Quinn was going to figure out what he knew and how it could be employed to make him look good.

"Wouldn't you rather take a seat in the living room, Chief Inspector?" Beverly asked.

Roy's eyes narrowed a little further. "No, dear. The chief inspector is just leaving." It was a challenge. "Unless you believe taking me into custody to get me to talk is a good idea?"

Chief Inspector Quinn stared back at the ageing RAF Wing Commander, his face emotionless and impossible to read.

"I don't know where Albert Smith is," Roy lied.

With a nod, Quinn took his hat back out from under his left arm.

"Very well, Wing Commander Hope," he replied, emphasising Roy's rank to make a point. "You can have it your way. Understand this though. The order to monitor your credit and bank cards came through an hour ago. Last night you booked a room at a small B&B in Eton, and you don't appear to be there. I wonder who is."

With that, the chief inspector backed out of the door and walked briskly back up the garden path to his waiting car and driver.

Closing his front door, Roy uttered a word that earned a scowl from his wife.

"I'll have to warn him," Roy grumbled, angry at himself for being caught so easily. He should have anticipated that the police might investigate Albert's friends and Roy had been with him right through the caper in Whitstable.

Little did he know that Albert had left his phone on charge in Edwina's house and wouldn't receive the warning until it was much, much too late.

Ringer

One side of the Wallace factory was dominated by an ageing painted sign. Reminding Albert of post war styles, the paint was faded but intact, displaying the family name in six-foot-high red letters captured within a blue border.

The factory sat at the end of a street of houses, filling the view as it stretched to the left and right.

Rex, keeping his thoughts to himself, and walking on Albert's far side to get as much space between him and Delilah as possible, was acutely aware of Eric's exuberance.

The young pup was straining at the end of his lead and overwhelmed with excitement.

Jessica was doing her best to keep him in check.

"Eric, calm down. What's the hurry?" She gave his lead a yank in the forlorn hope it might convince him to walk instead of ... whatever the heck it was he was trying to do now.

"Hey, Dad, look!" Eric barked at Rex. "I'm ahead! I'm ahead! Shall we have a race? I bet you can run really fast. I'm going to be a fast runner too. I'll show you just as soon as I get off this lead. Woah! Squirrel!"

Rex's ears pricked up at the mention of his most hated foe. He'd been doing his utmost to drown out Eric's constant need to make noise and questioned if he had ever been that annoying as a pup. He doubted it.

They were going somewhere, and his human seemed more distracted than usual. Something was bothering him, that was the conclusion Rex had reached though what it was remained a mystery. Ever since the order to give chase last night, Rex had been trying to figure out whether there was another crime to solve. He'd not witnessed one and still wasn't sure why his human had sent him after the couple last night.

Being a dog, he didn't dwell for long on such questions. There had been a lot of excitement recently, chases, explosions, a trip in a rather odd-looking car that then took to the sky ... Rex enjoyed it all. Well, maybe not the exploding beach part, that had been a little too close for comfort and made his ears ring. However, he got to do all these things with his human and that made them fun.

Whatever they were up to now, whether there was a mystery to solve or not, Rex would stand by the old man's side and be ready for action if he was needed.

All that notwithstanding, Delilah and Eric, who was still jabbering endlessly by the way, were a problem he needed to fix. The pattern of his recent life was to move somewhere new every few days. He certainly hoped that was going to be the case again this time. Worryingly though, Delilah made it sound as though they were staying with her for good.

Rex could remember the other human he used to live with, Albert's mate. She had died long enough ago that her scent has faded from his memory, and he'd not lived with her for long before she was gone. Was this something humans did? They lose one mate and after a time they find a replacement?

The squirrel Eric has spotted shot out from under a car a few yards ahead of them. Spotting the dogs, it froze for a half second on the pavement before bolting.

The half second was all the time the dogs needed, all three German Shepherds lunging forward to get to the cursed vermin. There was no decision to do so; the signal reaching their paws had bypassed their brains.

Albert had spotted the squirrel at the same time as his dog and opted to throw his weight in the opposite direction. It counteracted Rex's lunge, stopping the oversized dog before he could get moving.

Jessica wasn't so lucky.

With a dog lead in each hand, Jessica was almost yanked off her feet. Dressed for a day at the office, she wasn't attired for dog wrangling, but knew well enough the trials of taking a headstrong young dog anywhere, so her heels were in her handbag, and she had running shoes on her feet.

Nevertheless, the burst of energy from Delilah and Eric caught her by surprise and she pitched forward.

"SQUIRREL!" barked Eric, his paws scrambling madly to get purchase.

Jessica offered him an unladylike response and grabbed a handy lamppost to keep herself from falling.

Albert came to her aid, but by then she had the dogs back under control. They were thirty yards from the factory entrance and had come to rest opposite a small bakery. It had been formed in the converted downstairs of a terraced house. Albert had grown up seeing such businesses on a daily basis. The parade of shops in his hometown of East Malling was reduced to a newsagent now, where in his youth it had boasted a greengrocer, a butcher, a tobacconist, a hair salon ... Now the newsagent doubled as all of them except the salon.

The baker's shop had all manner of wares displayed in the window, though it was one item in particular that caught Albert's eye.

"I'm just going to grab something for my lunch," he announced, a little more deliberately than the situation required.

Still sorting Eric and Delilah out, Jessica turned her head to shoot Albert a questioning look.

"There'll be loads of craft food trucks at the open day. Wouldn't you rather get something hot? That's what I'm going to do."

Albert thought that sounded much better, but he needed an excuse to go into the bakery and it was too late to go back on his announcement now.

"Yes," he said, "I think I'll just get a sandwich anyway. Just in case. Do you want anything?"

Jessica shook her head and beckoned for Albert to hand over Rex's lead.

Inside the shop, Albert did as he claimed he would and bought a sandwich for his lunch. The bakery clearly made a killing selling freshly baked rolls, as they had a wide selection available in a display just inside the door.

Checking to make sure Jessica wasn't watching him – he found her to be checking her watch in an irritated fashion as if they were about to be late – and pointed to the glass fronted cabinet under the shop's counter.

"I'll take four of those, if I may."

The young man behind the counter carefully bagged up four items into a cardboard box and handed them over. Checking once again to see if Jessica was looking, Albert placed them into his backpack along with his sandwich and zipped it closed.

Paying cash so his card wouldn't show up on a police computer any-where, he strolled merrily and innocently from the shop.

"All done?" asked Jessica brightly as she offered Albert Rex's lead.

Eric was bouncing in place, eager to get going again.

Rex eyed his human, one eyebrow hiked high on his head.

"What have you got in the bag, old man?" he wanted to know. "Smells like something I would like to eat, that's for sure."

Noticing Rex's attention, Albert ruffled the fur on his skull and set off to cover the final yards toward the factory. He was feeling nervous, and he knew why - he was going up against the Gastrothief's agents again and they had proven themselves to be willing to kill. Would they know who he was? He expected to find out soon enough.

The bigger question though, now that he was thinking about it, was whether they would show today at all. They had targeted Jessica, of that he was certain, but she didn't seem to have any idea why. Some-thing about that was bothering him. The familiar feeling that he had missed a vital clue along the way refused to dissipate, but she was helping him to get into the factory and he had no reason to grill her on the subject. Not yet anyway.

A van drove by them as they walked through the pedestrian entrance to the side of the factory's impressive wrought iron gates, the sign written on its sides displayed the legend - 'Morton's Perfect Pies'.

It proved to be just one of a number of vehicles dotted around the courtyard of the factory where stallholders were in the throes of setting out their goods. Jessica had explained to Albert that this was an 'event' in the local calendar, but he'd failed to fully grasp just how big of an occasion it was.

A fluttering of nerves stole through his stomach when he saw the sign inviting Eton Mess contestants to register. It hung above a desk to the left which was in turn positioned directly in front of the entrance to a large white marquee.

Almost stuttering, Albert asked, "Is the competition going to be in there?"

Heading directly for the registration desk, Jessica nodded. "Yes. It used to be quite a small affair, but when that *Bake Off* show came on TV, someone got the idea of introducing this lavish marquee. You might think it's overkill, but they get twice as many visitors now and it's great for business. The open day makes far more profit than one might expect."

There wasn't exactly a queue at the desk, but there was a lady in front of them. Albert could hear her arguing from several yards away.

"I want to be at one of the tables near the front. You stuck me all the way in the back last year, and it cost me the title." The lady stood five feet and six inches tall with hair that was shot through with grey and held in place by an Alice band. Her brand new and pristine winter coat fell to mid-thigh where a black cotton skirt then continued the journey south to meet a pair of designer wellingtons.

Behind the desk a man in a suit was doing his best to remain polite. "I'm sorry, Mrs Medina, but the table assignments have already been made. I can assure you they were awarded randomly."

"Poppycock!" Mrs Medina retorted instantly.

Albert recognised both her voice and her tone from the telephone conversation last night. That it had not gone well was an understatement. He wanted to say something now, but couldn't come up with anything that was going to improve his chances of getting on her good side, until it occurred to him to question where he was going to be positioned.

Interrupting, Albert said, "You can swap with me if you like. That's assuming I have a more attractive table position. I really don't mind."

The man behind the table flicked his eyes away from Mrs Medina to look at Albert with a curt nod in Jessica's direction when he spotted her.

Mrs Medina, a scowl firmly in place on her forehead to give the impression it was a permanent feature swivelled around to see who had spoken.

"Who are you?" Mrs Medina demanded to know. "Why would you want to swap with me? Is this some sort of trick?"

Somewhat taken aback by her response, Albert did not get a chance to reply because Jessica was already speaking.

Addressing her work colleague behind the desk she said, "Jason Thomas, this is Albert Smith. He's the one I messaged you about last night."

Jason looked down at the clipboard positioned on the table surface in front of him, remarking after a moment, "Oh yes. The gentleman taking Mr Lawrence's place."

Mrs Medina's frown shot skyward when she heard Albert's name. "Albert Smith!" she exclaimed. "Albert Smith! You're the one who called me last night, trying to convince me there might be someone after me." Swivelling to jab a finger at Jason, she demanded, "I want the judges! I want them to disqualify this man. He's already employing dirty tactics to put off the bookies' favourite."

Jason sincerely doubted anyone was betting on the outcome of what was for everyone else, a fun competition. There wasn't even any prize money, yet this woman turned up year after year striving to win.

"I'm not calling the judges, Mrs Medina. You have your table assignment. Please either sign yourself in or move along so I can check in the other contestants."

Dismissed by Jason, who was already peering around her to address Albert, but refusing to let that be the end of it, Melissa levelled a fresh accusation.

"You've brought in a ringer then, have you? Arriving with the chief executive's assistant no less." She lifted a finger to prod Albert in the chest though she refrained from actually making physical contact.

"Who are you then? Some noted chef brought in specifically to ensure the trophy stays with the factory?" She dropped her accusing finger and stepped forward to get inside Albert's personal space. Almost touching him when she warned, "When I find out who you are, I'm going to expose this whole sordid shenanigan. It's a wonder I turn up at all. The judges are all crooked, you all go out of your way to make sure someone from the factory wins every year, and now you've brought in a ringer. Well, I'll not be fooled into taking your table, that's for certain." Snapping her head and eyes back around to stare accusingly at Jason behind the registration table, Mrs Medina signed where he indicated and without another word stomped into the marquee.

Questioning how it was that he was going to stay close to Melissa Medina *and* be able to intercept the Gastrothief's agents if they came for her, Albert was surprised to find Jason chuckling to himself.

Jessica asked, "Something amusing, Jason?"

He kept his pen on the clipboard and looked up at Albert with an apologetic expression.

"Good luck today."

Albert was about to question why it was that Jason's expression did not mirror his words when the man with the clipboard explained.

"I wish I was talking about the competition, but I'm afraid you probably have a greater challenge than that ahead of you." He struggled to keep the smirk from his face when he delivered the killer line. "Fate has decided to place you right next to Mrs Medina."

Jessica stepped in immediately. "Can't you move him somewhere else? The woman is clearly barmy."

Albert jumped in quick before Jason could do anything of the sort. "No, no. It's perfectly all right. It's not as if I *am* a ringer. She'll soon figure out I've got no idea what I'm doing and that should be the end of it."

With the matter settled, Jason asked Albert to sign himself in and gave him his table assignment. With Rex at his side, but not permitted inside the competition marquee, Albert moved away from the desk so the next person arriving behind him could register. His head was filled with questions about whether he would spot the Gastrothief's agents, and his eyes were roving the courtyard, lingering on anyone who closely matched either of the two figures he saw last night.

Jessica moved to join him, however a question from Jason stopped her.

"What are you doing here today anyway, Jessica? Is that your granddad or something? Only those involved with the open day have to be in today." Dropping his voice so he would not be overheard, he added, "I wouldn't be here if I didn't have to be."

Albert caught a flash of panic in Jessica's eye that she tried to hide by turning away.

"No, silly," she made it sound like Jason had got himself confused. "I'm heavily involved in running it."

Albert couldn't see Jessica's face, but he could see Jason's and his eyebrows were knitted in confusion now.

"But I thought …"

Jessica cut him off. "Trust me, Jason. I need to be here today." Giving him no further option to argue, she said, "Shouldn't you be attending to the next competition entrant?" before walking away.

Albert couldn't help but ask, "I thought you said you were running the whole thing?" It wasn't exactly a challenge; he didn't want to be rude to his host and helper, but there was something that just didn't add up about her and the clues were beginning to pile up.

She waved him off dismissively, "I exaggerated, Albert, that's all. I wasn't trying to big myself up or anything. I just didn't see that I needed to bore you with all the finite detail. Jason doesn't know that I'm involved in helping because I'm doing most of the organisation that goes on in the background. It's not glamorous, but someone has to do it. Now, how about if I show you where my office is so you'll know where to find me?"

Jessica, led by the dogs, took Albert into the factory's main building. It was an impressive brick structure that stretched the length of a football field and was full to the brim in every direction with machinery.

Looking in through a corridor of windows as they made their way to the offices, Albert noted how clean it all looked. The machinery was a mix of old and new, but all was maintained in a pristine condition, and the floor looked clean enough to eat off.

"We've been shut for two days following the discovery of Joseph's body. Today will be the first time the machines have had food passed through them since Thursday night. Of course, that's cost the firm a whole pile of money because many of the raw products have a limited shelf life."

Jessica babbled on knowledgably, explaining that the cleaning routine on the factory shopfloor had to be rigidly adhered to. The chemicals employed were expensive because they were approved for use with food and had to be disposed of under tight regulations.

Albert couldn't fathom why she was giving him so much information that had nothing to do with why he was here, and suspected it was so she would be talking and therefore he couldn't be.

Should he challenge her again? It would be rude to do so, specially since she had given him a believable response every time he had questioned her thus far. Telling himself to focus on the Gastrothief, Albert almost walked into Jessica when she stopped outside a door.

Albert saw when a man in an office beyond hers nodded his head at Jessica before returning to his work. Squinting his eyes to read at a distance, Albert noted that the man in his early fifties was the firm's chief executive. He was dressed like a politician in a smart blue suit and an Eton College tie. Some grey around his temples denoted the man's age and he looked stressed. Albert could imagine such a job would come with a good deal of pressure and thought nothing more of it as Jessica produced a key.

"This is my office," she announced. "I'll keep the dogs in here with me today. I have plenty to do, and some of that is outside, so I'll be sure to take them with me. I'll text you when I do, so you can pop out and see Rex."

At the sound of his name, Rex looked up. His nose was working overtime sampling the air and questioning what he could smell.

Albert twitched and groaned. At the mention of his phone, he had moved his hand to pat the pocket where he kept it, but before his arm had moved a few inches, he realised he didn't have it.

"My phone is still on charge in your kitchen," he sighed, hanging his head.

His announcement gave Jessica pause, but only for a second. "Okay, not to worry. Gran is coming along later anyway. I'll get her to drop it off."

Albert made his facial muscles go still so he wouldn't show his distaste for Jessica's solution.

"Super," he replied, thinking it was nothing of the sort.

Putting her handbag down, Jessica returned to the door. "Stay here, dogs," she commanded, showing them the palm of her hand. "I'll be back in a few minutes."

"We're going down to the marquee now?" Albert sought to confirm.

"Yes. That's what you want, isn't it?"

117

"I'd like to see where Mr Lawrence met his end first, if that's okay. I assume the factory tours will be later, so we'll have the place to ourselves if we go now, yes?"

Jessica nodded her head. "You think the agents of the Gastrothief will show today?"

Albert wanted to respond in a highly positive manner, but the truth was that he had no idea if they would or not. All he could do was hope. If he was right, and they wanted to capture someone to make Eton Mess, then here and today was the ideal opportunity. Why else would they be here?

Watching the humans depart, Rex sniffed the air again, and murmured to himself, "They've been here already."

The Gastrothief

Many miles from Albert's current location, Earl Bacon surveyed his underground habitat. Built in secret in a cavern beneath a small hill in Wales, it was the size of a small village and housed almost two hundred people.

It had cost almost every last penny of his family fortune, but what concern was money when the world was going to end? Armageddon was a subject over which the earl had obsessed since he was a young boy. The news stories of global warming, melting icecaps, chemical pollution poisoning the oceans, critically endangered species going extinct in droves despite humanity's best efforts, the loss of the rainforests, and more all added up to what he considered to be a certain and inescapable future.

His underground lair would keep him safe, and with him those who he had chosen to save. That 'the chosen' continued to complain about their captivity was a source of great irritation to the earl. He'd explained many times that leaving his underground facility would result in their death, yet still they wanted to leave.

The ones with children were the worst.

Regardless, no one was going anywhere. If the world at large found out about his facility, they would all want to get inside once the penny finally dropped on their impending doom. His shelter was fortified, of course, but not to the point where he had an army to defend against invaders. The main entrance was protected by a six-inch-thick steel door, an item the earl purchased from the British military when they were shutting down old barracks in Northern Ireland. He'd bought it for a song, the fools selling it to him as scrap.

However, it wasn't the only way in or out. Fresh water filtering through the rock above had been channelled into a small river and then a lake which had been stocked with plentiful shoals of fish. Naturally, where water flowed in, it had to also flow out, and there had been two deaths from among his 'chosen' as they attempted to escape underwater. Theoretically, it was also possible to get out through the air scrubber. Such a feat would require some dismantling before access to the surface could be gained, but the earl was far more concerned about the people on the outside getting in.

When global crops began to fail and livestock starved, worldwide famine would break out and only those with the foresight to prepare themselves would survive. That was the purpose of all his effort - to survive.

And since he intended to survive, he was going to do so in comfort. The accommodation for his 'chosen' was meagre, especially when compared with his own palatial surroundings, but the real difference between master and servants was the food.

The Earl dined on only the finest delicacies from around the world. Most of it came from his beloved home nation of Great Britain, and he had amassed huge stockpiles of those foods that he wanted most of all. The thought of running out of caviar was enough to break him out in a cold sweat, but obtaining the foods he wanted had proven to be easier than he'd anticipated.

Employing criminals with few or zero morals to carry out his dirty work was little different from taking out an ad in a newspaper. Once he found the first person, the rest came from known contacts.

One of his employees, an attractive woman called Tanya, was at that moment waiting upon an answer from the Earl. He'd been deliberating his response for more than a minute already.

Finally, he said, "No, Tanya, I want you to focus on Albert Smith and that wretched dog of his. Find him, kill the dog, and bring Albert Smith to me."

"He's not working for or with the police," Tanya pointed out, not for the first time. "There is a warrant out for his arrest and there is some idiot chief inspector in Kent who is acting as if Albert Smith was behind the explosion in Whitstable."

"Be that as it may, but I want to know who he is working for. It cannot be blind chance that one man keeps cropping up to ruin my plans. He was in Stilton. He was in Biggleswade. He was in Arbroath. I need to know how it is that he keeps appearing in the exact place and at the exact time as my agents. He killed Eugene and Frances, and now you tell me that Baldwin is dead too?"

Tanya did not bother to reiterate her version of events. The truth was that she had killed Baldwin, but Albert Smith's giant dog had left her partner with injuries that would have required hospitalisation. Baldwin would have recovered, and nobody would have questioned whatever story they concocted to explain the wounds – '*A dog ran out of the woods and bit me before running off again*'. So it was for her own gain that she murdered her partner. She wanted to work with someone new. What she did not want to do was go after Albert Smith.

"He will recognise me," she expressed what she felt was a pertinent point. "It would be safer and more expedient to send someone else. I am due to be in Cornwall tonight. I have done the research. Let me take Kelly with me and we'll return with that which you prize."

Tanya fully expected the earl to comply with her request; he had demonstrated a willingness to listen to her advice and, in general, treated her as if she was a trusted advisor. So it came as something of a shock when he immediately refused.

"I have already sent Kelly to Cornwall along with Liam. They have proven quite capable in recent months. I want you to focus on Albert Smith. No one else in my employ has seen him in the flesh. Go now, and do not return until you have him."

Tanya cocked a hip and levelled an even stare at the Earl.

"This is not a task that I am happy to perform. I will need a new partner and I expect to be suitably compensated."

A snort of laughter escaped the Earl's bulbous nose. "Shall we say a hundred thousand pounds, Tanya?" That so many of his employees still couldn't grasp that money would shortly be of no use to anyone continued to amuse him. He was more than happy to fritter away his last millions - what was the point in keeping it?

Failing to hide her excitement at the enormous figure the earl offered, Tanya fought to rein her smile under control.

"And a partner?" she prompted.

Turning away from one of his lead assassins and collecting the small bell from the table beside his chair, he said, "Take whomever you wish, provided they are not already assigned to another task." Then, his brain filled only with thoughts of food, he rang the bell to summon his butler.

Albert Smith had started out as nothing more than a fly in the ointment, but now he had become something else. According to Tanya, the old man and his giant dog had almost caught her and Baldwin in Kent. He had to be stopped.

Impatiently, he gave the bell another shake, this time with more vigour. That damned interfering old busybody was giving the earl indigestion, and nothing upset him more than being put off his food.

Difficult Balance

"What are you doing? What are you doing? What are you doing?" Eric was bouncing about on his paws with such exuberance and energy that to Rex's mind it looked as if the young pup was standing on an electrified floor.

"I'm comparing scents," Rex replied, his voice calm and quiet as if that might have any impact on the young dog.

"Ooooh, why? What's going on?" Eric begged to know.

With his eyes closed and trying his hardest to filter out input from all his other senses, Rex zeroed in on the combination of smells he wanted to examine. Unfortunately, this left him open to attack.

"Plaaaahrk!" Rex shook his head and used a front paw to swipe at his right ear where Eric had just sucked on it.

"What's going on, Dad? What's going on? Is there something exciting to do? Is there? Is there? Is there?"

"Leave your father be now, Eric," Delilah cooed from her position just a few feet away where she had been watching the exchange.

Rex had to fight not to bark when he said, "I'm not his father. I only met you yesterday."

"But you want the role, and that's good enough for me, lover," Delilah murmured sexily as she rolled onto her side to offer Rex a promise-laden smile.

Rex had no training for such situations. He didn't wish to brag, but he'd met plenty of lady dogs in the past, many of whom had been accommodating to his desires because, driven by biology, theirs had been greater than his. What he knew for certain, was that Delilah was offering something that was hard to come by and he wanted it. Hard wired instructions at the back of his brain demanded he complied with all her demands so that the mating could continue.

Nevertheless, he found himself fighting it because it felt like such a trap.

Unable to figure out what he could do to quell her advances, especially now that he had already committed the deed several times, Rex focused instead on the problem in hand.

Speaking to Eric, he explained, "My human sent me to chase two people last night. I believe it's a safe assumption that they are criminals of some kind."

Eric gasped, his eyes filled with awe, and Rex pressed on before the pup could interrupt him.

"I'm not sure what crime they might have committed, however my human has shown himself to be quite adept, so I'm willing to give him the benefit of the doubt. If I assume that they're up to something, then I am duty bound to investigate. The old man does okay by himself, but I don't think he would ever solve a case without me there to nudge him along. The same couple I chased last night have been in this office recently. Not today," Rex decided, "but in the last couple of days to be sure."

"Wow," Eric's mouth was hanging open. "You are amazing! So what do we do now? Do we go and get them?" The younger dog's top lip curled upwards to reveal his teeth in a display of bravery. "I'll help you get them. Just show me where they are!"

"Steady there," Rex laughed. "We can't get out of this room," he nudged the door with his head and pawed at the door to check he wasn't overstating their situation. "That's something we will have to overcome. Your human claimed she wouldn't be long. I guess we'll see how soon she returns and if she is willing to listen."

Eric tilted his head to one side. "To listen? You can talk to humans?"

Rex sputtered as a laugh burst from his lips.

"No, pup. I cannot, but let me tell you a story about a bulldog and a cat I met just yesterday ..."

The Factory

Their footsteps echoed in the empty factory and the enormous space gave his voice an odd, intrusive quality when Albert spoke.

"The report said he was found in the morning when the early shift came in."

"That's right," Jessica indicated a direction for Albert to go – the factory was a maze of walkways between and over the machinery that would confuse new workers for weeks until they found their way around, Albert assessed. "They ran up the boxing machine and a warning light came on instantly. Joseph was lodged down in the bottom. It was clear he had fallen from the maintenance walkway above, but no one can figure out what he was doing up there."

"Did they determine the time of death?"

Jessica pursed her lips, answering Albert's questions because she needed to keep him on side. She was going to use the poor deluded sap to create a distraction and to cover her escape if needed. His screwball story about a master criminal had played right into her hands. If he wanted to tell himself he was here to catch people in the act of kidnapping a talented chef or some other nonsense, then she was fine with that.

However, she was nervous about what she was doing and trying hard not to let it show. Coming back here at all was a risk, but she was more motivated to find the truth than ever before, Joseph's death had seen to that.

Because it was her fault.

Not that she had killed him, but it was her carefully whispered words that had sent him snooping, and she was sure that had resulted in his death. Albert claimed he interrupted a couple who were about to attack her last night. Okay, so he believed they were there as part of his crazy Gastrothief thing, but even though that was silly, Jessica believed he was right about their intentions.

When she discovered Joseph's 'accident' her first act had been to attempt to access the same files Joseph had assured her he was going to inspect. He hadn't told her he was going to do it at night. He also hadn't told her it was going to get him killed, but that was probably because he had no idea.

Whoever the couple was, they would be back. If they were trying to get her in the street last night, surely they would attempt to reacquire her today. If accessing or downloading the data was what got Joseph caught and sent them after her when she tried to do it, then she was shortly to kick the hornets' nest again.

One last shot. That's what she told herself. Get the data she needed today, now that she believed it was here, and then get out. The old man would be looking for the couple, so if they showed up looking for her, she would make sure he tried to do whatever it was the crazy old man had planned.

Conscious she hadn't responded to his last question about when Joseph died, she said, "I'm not sure," adding, "If they did, they didn't tell us. It had to have been between seven when the last of the cleaning crew would have left, and six the next morning when people started to arrive. My guess would be it was not long after the building was locked up."

A frown arrived on Albert's forehead. "You appear to have given this some thought."

"Oh, not really," Jessica's reply sounded reactive because it was. *The old man was asking too many questions.*

Albert picked at another loose thread. "Surely there would be security camera footage? If this place doesn't employ security guards to keep it safe at night, then it must have a security firm monitoring the place." Even while saying it, his mind cast back to the Porker factory in Reculver and how the Gastrothief's agents had obtained the information they needed to get in without being caught. They'd taken equipment and people and then set a fire to cover their tracks.

Jessica pointed to the left. "It's just down here," she announced, conveniently not answering Albert's question.

At a galvanised steel cat ladder, Jessica grabbed a rung above her head and was about to climb when Albert noisily cleared his throat.

"Do you, ah, think perhaps I should go first?" he asked, pointedly.

With her eyebrows waggling and trying to unpick the secret meaning behind his question, Jessica asked, "No, why?"

His cheeks tinging slightly, Albert did his best to not look at her when he said, "Um, well, you're wearing a dress, my dear." Jessica's misunderstanding deepened. "And well, you'll be above me. And I'll ... well, I'll be looking up," he mimed where his eyes would be while ascending the ladder.

Joining Albert in blushing, Jessica moved out of the way so Albert could go up first.

At the top of the ladder, Albert reached a walkway that ran between the machines.

Arriving behind him, Jessica was already talking. "Milk is pumped into the machine from tanks outside. The factory gets a fresh delivery every day. It arrives in the churner ..." she indicated what appeared to be a giant bowl with an equally giant paddle thingy in its centre, "where computers monitor the consistency and deliver it under pressure to the assembly line."

Albert looked over the railing. It was twenty feet to the base of the machine into which Joseph Lawrence had allegedly fallen. Such a fall would injure a man for sure, but Albert expected nineteen out of twenty would survive. Perhaps Joseph had just been unlucky. Perhaps he was pushed into the machine with his neck already broken, the accident intended to cover up his murder.

Albert considered the idea for a moment and dismissed it. Were it the case that the Gastrothief's agents had accidentally killed Joseph - the one with the flat top looked capable of snapping a neck - then they would have removed the body and all trace that anything had happened.

No, Joseph had been trying to escape and had fallen. Albert was more certain than ever now that he was going to be able to trap two of the Gastrothief's top people today. They would return to obtain that which their boss sought, and he would make sure Rex cornered them when they did.

The police would come, and it would all come out in the confusion that followed.

The Pension Fund

Chrissy and Kasper had already returned to the factory, or at least to its general vicinity. Unable to get in because the gates were closed to control the crowd already queuing for the open day, they joined the line of people snaking along the side of the factory wall.

Their appearances were completely changed from the previous evening, most notably that of Chrissy who harboured a secret few knew.

Dressed as a man again, her meagre chest was hidden beneath a spandex binder designed to create a masculine profile. Her hair, always short and usually spiky, was flat and combed with a side parting in a traditional man's style. With glasses, men's clothing, and a pair of boots to make her feet look bigger than the size two they were, she knew no one would believe they were looking at a woman.

It was in her early teens when she began to identify as gender non-conforming. Prior to that, her life had been a confusing mess, most especially at the onset of puberty when her parents expected her to look like all her friends and be interested in boys and makeup et cetera.

Now, given her line of work, switching from one gender to the other gave her an added level of anonymity.

Kasper's flat top hair was gone, and the slick combed back style he now sported had changed from blonde to a dark brown. Clad in a smart suit, he looked every bit the powerful businessman he wanted people to see and remember.

They needed to acquire Jessica Fletcher today, and there was no option for failure. However, their plan to snatch her as she walked to work was scuppered before it could be given life. Not only did she have company, which was not her routine, but she had not one but two large dogs and a puppy with her.

The old man, assumed to be a chance encounter last night - nothing more than the wrong person in the wrong place at the wrong time - was back and it was almost as if he were acting as their target's bodyguard.

An old man wasn't going to be a problem, Kasper could knock him out and his body would vanish along with the woman's once the boss was done with her, but the three dogs? They were a barrier to success.

Unless they were to adopt a full-frontal attack with weapons as their strategy – one that was sure to draw the police, they were going to have to rethink.

They were doing precisely that when the boss called for an update.

"Why have you not called to tell me that you have her?" he enquired the moment the call connected. His voice dripped with honey like a sticky trap.

Cursing in her head, Chrissy replied, "We will have her soon. The plan to take her before she got to work was compromised."

"Compromised?"

Chrissy blew out a hard breath of frustration and told him the truth.

"The old man was with her again."

"The old man? The same old man you assured me was nothing more than an unfortunate and unpredictable factor that prevented you taking Miss Fletcher last night?" Again, the voice in her ear was laced with sugar, but she could hear the pressure building and knew it was going to blow soon.

"Yes. The same old man. He is not a problem, but the target is moving with three large German Shepherd dogs." She chose to omit the part about one being a puppy still, "A change of strategy is required, nothing more."

As expected, when her employer spoke again, it was a roar that forced her to move the phone away from her ear.

"You are ruining my morning! This is a simple job! I made my name doing simple jobs like the one I gave you!"

It was true she knew. Her employer was known for his brutal violence and rate of success. It was how he came to leverage his way up the chain and now he operated as a separate entity from those who once employed him, offering a service the underworld of criminals needed.

The call ended with a final banshee shriek to not fail again, and Percy Crumley drew back his arm to launch his phone across his open plan living space.

His perfectly poached eggs had gone cold during the exchange, and he was upset about that too. Slowly lowering his arm with the phone still gripped in his giant fist, he sucked in a deep breath through his nose and forced the rage inside to subside.

It was time to enact an emergency plan. The Eton Mess factory had provided a lucrative and above all safe means through which he could launder money. For years no one had looked twice at it. He operated the same system at dozens of large firms across this and the surrounding countries, finding men he could carefully lean on to make some extra money without having to lift a finger.

All the firm needed was a privately run pension fund and a boss motivated by greed. Unsurprisingly, there were lots of those to pick from.

Money made illegally through criminal enterprises would move through each company's books, arriving in the pension fund to be paid to former employees. That the payees were either deceased, the fictitious spouses of deceased employees, or even just fictitious employees, had never been detected and never would be. Over a year, through dozens of firms, Percy Crumley laundered close to nine figures of money that the tax man never saw a penny of.

The money would vanish from each pension fund in a seemingly legitimate manner only to arrive in a series of accounts from which Percy then withdrew.

He was lauded by his clients who had no idea how he operated such a slick system. He would never tell them, of course. He simply deducted his five percent and enjoyed his life.

Now though, he could feel the devil nipping at his toes. Joseph Lawrence, an absolute nobody who worked in the health and safety department at Wallace's, had accessed the encrypted data file where the pension fund transactions were hidden.

Joseph Lawrence's actions triggered an alarm at Percy's end; a two-layer system designed to give him peace of mind. Simply accessing the data was enough to condemn him, and the moment his accountants advised him of the breach, Percy sent Chrissy and her giant, monosyllabic partner, Kasper, to collect the man.

Mr Lawrence was there in the middle of the night; a sure sign he knew what he was doing. Percy felt certain he was going to discover the man was a mole, embedded in the firm recently by Her Majesty's Revenue and Customs. He wasn't though, he was just a guy from health and safety, but the chance to quiz him was lost because Chrissy and Kasper managed to kill him. That he accidentally fell to his death was neither here nor there, for the result was the same.

Then a second breach a day later, this time from the desk of the CEO's new assistant, well that was too much. That she now had protection and was going back to work ... it was time to enact an emergency response.

He would pull the funds, that would stop the woman from obtaining them. Perhaps she didn't understand why she couldn't get to them last time and maybe she would have figured it out. Removing the money and all trace it was ever there could be done in seconds. The staff at the factory would wonder what had happened to their pension fund but that was no concern of his. They would turn to the CEO for an explanation, and he would not be able to give one because he would be dead.

That was a necessary step to remove any chance of discovery. Enough of the fund – his share for this quarter, in fact, for it was a small price to pay – would be discovered in the CEO's bank account and a suicide note next to the greedy fool's body would be enough to confuse and convince the investigating officers to look no further.

Dropping his reading glasses into place so that he could see the screen on his phone, Percy Crumley brought up his contacts list and from it selected Oliver Walsh, the current chief executive officer of Wallace's.

While the phone rang in his ear, Percy considered how a person like Mr Walsh might choose to commit suicide.

The Competition Floor

I n the marquee, Albert's eyes flared at the rows of tables set out
for the contestants. There were ... he counted ... eighty of them.
The tables were set up with a set of kitchen scales, some bowls and
basic utensils, plus a small refrigerator and an oven beneath. They were
arranged in rows along the far wall of the marquee. To his right at
one short end was a small, raised stage that could be more accurately
described as a dais. Behind it curtains hid from sight what Albert
imagined was an admin area. Opposite the contestants' tables, where
he was standing now, was a plastic barrier to corral the audience and it
all surrounded an open area in the middle.

Albert swallowed hard.

Most of the tables already had a contestant behind or near them; people unpacking their ingredients and loading them into the refrigerator. No one was doing any preparation yet – the contest wasn't starting until ten o'clock, and judges/officials were moving between the tables, beady eyes scrutinising what they were seeing.

"This is all a little more serious than I anticipated," he squeaked. There were few things in the world that scared Albert, but mixing ingredients and putting them in an oven to produce food was one that always brought him out in a cold sweat. "This might not have been such a good idea."

Sensing that her distraction tactic was about to reverse out of the marquee, Jessica placed a hand against the small of his back. She needed him.

"It will be fine, Albert. There're so many contestants here, no one will notice what you are up to."

"But I'm supposed to make a meringue," Albert gibbered. "That's right, isn't it? That's what the crunchy white stuff is called."

Jessica pulled a face. Albert had said he wasn't particularly adept in the kitchen, but she hadn't appreciated just how limited his skills were. In fact, she had assumed he was being modest.

Reaching into her handbag, she said, "I tell you what I'll do, I'll write a few instructions down for you to follow. I'm fairly sure there's nothing against that in the rules. The meringue is the hardest part of it, after all. If you get that bit right, the rest of it should be easy."

Albert's eyes were showing altogether too much white for her liking. Tearing off a page of hastily scribbled instruction, she handed it over to be sure that he understood what it said.

Fumbling to find his reading glasses, Albert squinted at the page. His initial burst of uncharacteristic panic had subsided when he reminded himself that it really didn't matter whether he did a terrible job or not. He was not here to compete. More than anything, his purpose today was to watch Melissa Medina and be ready.

It was at that precise moment when a major flaw in the plan occurred to him. They wouldn't come for her in public, or at least they wouldn't do so visibly, but that didn't mean they would not attempt some form of subterfuge to lure her away. If that happened, what was it that he proposed to do about it?

The entirety of his plan was to have Rex intervene. Maybe it would be tonight when they came for her, maybe it would be tomorrow. Maybe someone else would win today's competition and he would find that he was protecting the wrong target.

Whoever they chose to snatch, later would be better, because he needed Rex at his side.

Breaking his train of thought, Jessica nudged his arm and pointed to an as yet unoccupied table.

"We should get your things unpacked and into the fridge," she prompted.

Following Jessica across the marquee, Albert spotted Mrs Medina when she rose from behind her table. In her hands, freshly unpacked from the box it came in no doubt, was an elegant white marble lazy Susan.

She placed it on her table and stepped back to admire it. Not content, she moved it half an inch to the left, and gave a prim nod to herself when she was happy.

"Hello again," Albert hallooed her. He was at his table now and just a few feet from her. He added a friendly wave, believing it would be much easier to stick close and watch her if they were on speaking terms.

The smile on Melissa Medina's face froze then fell, her eyes taking on a pinched expression when she squinted back at Albert.

"You again," she remarked coldly. "Why don't you tell me your real name? Then I can look you up and find out what restaurant you work for. Is it the Savoy in London? The Ritz? Are you a star on the Paris food circuit? Is that who they brought along to make sure I didn't win this year?"

Albert tried to fight the laugh that burst from his lips, but he simply couldn't manage it.

"My dear lady, I barely know one end of a spatula from another." Quickly juggling his backpack to put it down, he showed her the handwritten instructions for making meringue. "I'll bet you don't have instructions for how to make stuff."

Melissa's narrow-eyed expression remained in place. "Don't want to tell me your real name, eh?"

Hoping that this was an opening, Albert advanced upon her with his right hand extended.

"Roy Hope," he announced gamely. However, instead of taking his hand, a woman who was fast becoming his arch nemesis, was tapping away on her phone.

"Roy Hope," she muttered under her breath. "Sounds like the name of a three-star Michelin chef if ever I heard one."

Certain she wasn't going to find a picture, file, or record that married up his face with the name he had just given, Albert wasn't sure what she would think of that. Accepting defeat for now, he returned to his table where Jessica had finished placing his perishable items into the refrigerator.

"The competition starts in twenty minutes, Albert. The prize is awarded to the overall best Eton Mess pudding, and as I explained already, you have to make four because there are points awarded for presentation - they expect them all to be the same."

Unthinkingly, Albert inquired, "What are the other points awarded for?"

Using her left hand to count them off with her right index finger, Jessica recited, "Overall taste, tartness of fruit, crispness of meringue, and ten percent of the score is awarded for originality."

"Originality? I thought an Eton Mess was an Eton Mess? Surely if someone does something different it is no longer an Eton Mess and should be disqualified?"

Jessica shrugged, "I guess that is a difficult one to play." With a check of her watch, she said, "I really must be going. I don't want to leave Eric for too long. He's house trained, but a little forgetful. I'll need to fetch Mr Walsh too and make sure he's ready. He's starting this event and straight after that opening the main gates and welcoming the visitors."

Albert dipped his head in acknowledgement, letting Jessica go. As she bustled away, dodging around the people in the marquee to get to the exit, he looked down at his table and re-read the instructions for making a meringue.

All around him the other contestants were busy doing something. Most were wearing aprons and engaged in setting out little packets and bottles - ingredients to be incorporated in their dish.

Feeling bewildered, Albert wandered over to the marquee entrance and peered outside. A small crowd had gathered outside the gates waiting to be let in. Remembering how he and Jessica had gained entry through a side gate, it occurred to him that the Gastrothief's agents might be playing the role of visitors to the factory so they could mingle with the crowd arriving to enjoy the open day.

With hastened steps, he crossed to a position near the large wrought iron gates. He was looking for someone tall - the man with the flat top. The second figure from last night was shorter and would be almost impossible to pick out among the press of people, but to Albert's disappointment, there was no sign of either person.

Looking down the line, he could see only one man who was tall enough, though it wasn't the one he wanted. This man's hair was a different colour and style, and he was wearing a suit.

Huffing his frustration, Albert returned to the marquee.

Under the Table

Oliver Walsh could feel his stomach muscles knotting. He didn't think he'd ever felt this sick before in his life. His right hand was shaking when he placed his mobile phone on the surface of his desk.

A fast glance in the direction of Jessica's office was followed by a moment of relief when he discovered she was not there to observe his current state.

He had just endured his third phone conversation with Percy Crumley in forty-eight hours. The problem, Oliver acknowledged to himself, was that once one made a deal with the devil, there simply was no way to back out of it.

It was such a harmless thing he was doing. Oh, it was highly illegal, obviously, but it was also a victimless crime so far as he could see. Money came in and money went out. Where it came from and where it went was really none of his business. Oliver was far more interested in the fat sum that appeared in his own bank account each month; his fee for allowing the victimless system to operate and for ensuring that no one else knew about it.

It was the last part that bothered him most right now. Percy Crumley had been quite graphic in describing the penalty for allowing the movement of funds to be discovered and that was precisely what had happened.

Oliver could not explain it. In fact, he had no idea at all how it could be that Joseph Lawrence came to access the encrypted files. It was only accessible from one computer in the entire firm - the chief executive's which was located securely in the chief executive's office. His office. Not only that, one had to have the access code which Oliver kept in his head.

Well, okay, so he kept a copy on an old business card tucked inside his wallet even though Mr Crumley had told him to never write it down. It was ten digits for goodness sake! How was he supposed to remember that? It wasn't as if he needed to access the files ever. It was there only so he could do something for Mr Crumley at his request. Of course, when another opportunity popped up a couple of years after Percy Crumley came into Oliver's life, he chose to hide the data for it inside the same encrypted file system.

Together, his two under-the-table enterprises made him more money than his job at Wallace's. Not even his wife knew about the extra money and most of it had gone into secret offshore bank accounts.

Panicking when he got the first call from Mr Crumley, Oliver had rushed to find his wallet, holding his breath until with a relieved sigh, he found the old business card still where it had always been. He'd destroyed it right there and then, tearing it up and then burning it on the hob in his kitchen.

Regardless that Oliver still had the card, Joseph had re-entered the factory after business hours, picked the lock or otherwise found a method by which he could enter his boss's office, and then proceeded to find files that Oliver was convinced no one else even knew about. Somehow Joseph had the ten-digit access code.

Percy Crumley had called Oliver at home within minutes of the breach, demanding that he confirm he was not the one accessing the files, and then proceeded to scream at him with all manner of vile threats. Oliver promised to race to the factory so that he might catch whoever was behind it only to be threatened again and ordered to do nothing whatsoever. Percy Crumley had his own people, and they were taking care of it.

When he arrived at work the following morning, doing everything he could to act natural, even though his heart was racing, Oliver was shocked beyond words when he heard that Joseph Lawrence had been found dead inside the boxing machine.

Mr Crumley's people had found him, and they had killed him, of that Oliver was certain.

All day Friday, his heart refused to return to a normal rhythm. The clock ticked louder than it ever had before, and he waited for a phone call that didn't come.

Was Percy Crumley going to do anything?

Almost all the staff were sent home; it wasn't as if they could operate the factory anyway. Senior management had remained behind, and even though Oliver attempted to send Jessica away, his assistant, a relatively new but thoroughly efficient member of staff, insisted on staying. He dealt with the police, talked to the factory employees, and spent the entire day wondering if his car would explode when he got in it.

It didn't, and later that evening, when he had convinced himself that Joseph's interference was nothing more than an odd quirk of fate, his phone rang again.

There had been another breach. Someone else had attempted to access the encrypted files, only this time they were not doing it from Oliver's computer.

No, the person who had logged in was using his ten-digit access code, but had done so from Jessica Fletcher's terminal and used her password. Oliver wanted to confront her about it, but to do so would be to admit that he was complicit in Percy Crumley's operation. He had no choice but to bite his lip. Percy Crumley's people were going to deal with her too and there was nothing he could do about it.

He was shocked when she strolled into work this morning. She had an old man with her, who Oliver assumed was her grandfather. They hadn't dealt with her and that couldn't be good.

Now Percy wanted Oliver to go home and wait for him there. He refused to say why and wouldn't listen to Oliver's insistence that he needed to remain at the open day - he was supposed to address the crowd shortly.

Well, Oliver wasn't going home. He'd been worried that one day something like this might happen. He had no children and could always find a new wife, so he was going to get in his car, drive to the airport, and vanish for good.

With his passport in his hand, and his car keys in his pocket, the only other thing in the world that he needed was a credit card, and he had plenty of those. He would access the money in his offshore accounts once he got to wherever he was going, and he rather liked that he didn't know where that was. Furthermore, as he walked out of his office, he could feel an enormous burden lifting from his shoulders and it had nothing to do with Percy Crumley and his money. It was all to do with his other venture.

He couldn't say that it had kept him awake at night, but were he to ever have been caught, the public shame would have been terrible. Now he didn't have to worry and that felt great.

There was one last thing he needed to do on his way out the door: lie to Jessica that he had a family emergency and needed to pop home. No one would argue, he was the chief executive after all. Stanley Barrowman would step in to fill his shoes without a moment's thought. He'd wanted the job for years and was quite a capable fellow if a little unimaginative.

Imagining straightlaced Stanley discovering all that Oliver had been up to at the firm, a smile creased Oliver's face.

Feeling better already now that he'd chosen a course of action, the chief executive officer all but jogged to get to Jessica's door.

Thrusting it open, he made sure that his face looked suitably concerned again as he readied his lie.

Rex's Apprentice

"**F**reedom!"

Eric's loud and unexpected bark woke Rex. He'd talked for a while, telling the young pup about the crazy bulldog he'd met and the cat the bulldog had to live with. Doing so involved regaling Eric with the adventure they'd shared and that led to Rex falling down a rabbit hole of stories from his travels around the country with Albert.

By the time he'd finished, Eric wanted to fight seagulls, chase alley cats, lead a giant pack of dogs to victory over an evil criminal empire, and have something cool to say when it was done. The young pup's excitement level was overflowing, and he was becoming agitated by their confinement.

Delilah had done what most dogs do when there is nothing more interesting on offer – she went to sleep.

When he ran out of stories to tell, Rex found a spot next to the desk and laid his head down too. Sleep came easily, but no more than a few minutes later, his eyes snapped open to see Eric barging through the barely open door.

There was a man outside looking in, his face a mixture of shock and something else. He smelled of fear, a distinct scent all humans give out when terror grips them, and it made Rex leap to his feet.

The man was trying to shut the door again, but Eric was gone. In a snap decision, Rex went after him.

"Eric!" Rex barked as he shunted the door back six inches with his head. "Eric! Wait!"

Rex had no idea who the man was. He wore a suit, and his scent permeated the building so Rex assumed he belonged here. Whoever he was, he made one feeble attempt at grabbing Rex's collar. Rex slipped free and ran after the pup.

Behind him, Delilah barked, "Rex!" and he looked back to find she was trapped inside the office. Standing on her back legs, she was looking through the glass panels that made up the walls. "Get Eric. Don't let him get into any trouble! Be a father!"

She couldn't get out; the man in the suit had finally closed the door and was hurrying away in the opposite direction.

Harrumphing once again that he was not Eric's father, Rex nevertheless chased after him.

"Slow down, Pup."

"Gonna catch some bad guys!" Eric's voice rang back through the corridors.

He was easy to track; Rex could have found the young dog blindfolded, but inevitably, Rex caught up to him when Eric met with a closed door.

"How do we get out?" Eric barked, his enthusiasm boiling over.

Despite himself, Rex was starting to like the pup. It was like having an apprentice or a sidekick – someone to train.

Attempting to instil some calm, Rex parked his backend on the floor.

"We ought to return to the office. Your mum is still inside, and your human will be back soon, I'm sure. That's what she said ..."

Eric cut him off. "But you said you could smell the people you chased last night. That was what you said."

"Well, yes ..."

"And you said your human thought they were up to no good and that he always needs your help to solve the crimes you come across."

Rex couldn't deny it. "I did say that but ..."

"Then isn't it our duty as dogs to help now?" Eric had tilted his head and was staring at Rex with his face at an angle. Changing his voice, softening it so it sounded like he was pleading. "I want to help you catch the bad people, Dad."

How was he supposed to argue with that?

Rex drew in a slow, deep breath, filling his lungs while inside his head he argued about what the most sensible course of action might be. The safe play was to take Eric back to the office and wait outside for Eric's human to return. It was obvious though that Eric would resist; he wanted action and adventure.

The pup also made a good point: Rex's human was acting as if there was a crime to investigate and if he was right then the same people Rex chased last night were back here now and that had to mean they were after Eric's human.

That's who they were close to last night. Rex hadn't witnessed them doing anything that he saw as a crime, but he was willing to give his human the benefit of the doubt, the old man had earned it.

What then? What should he do? If Eric's human was in danger and she wasn't here – she'd already been gone longer than Rex expected, then he needed to find her. That was the right course of action.

Jumping back to his paws with an exaggerated flex of muscle that made Eric flinch and say, "Whoa," in an awe-filled manner, Rex double pumped his eyebrows and twitched his head to make the pup follow.

"There's a way out back here."

Who's in Charge?

In the marquee, the contestants were muttering. The competition was due to start in two minutes, five minutes before the gate opened, but no one had addressed the assembled amateur chefs yet.

Albert could hear what the people around him were saying: that the organisation this year was shoddy, and someone ought to be for the high jump.

A trio of concerned-looking staff from the factory, two men and a woman in smart, but casual office wear, were gathered near to the judging dais and a microphone on a stand. They looked to be arguing, but were doing so quietly so that no one could hear them.

Some of the contestants were hovering just a few yards away doing much the same and Albert questioned what they were doing for a second until it dawned on him – they were trying to decide who was going to ask what was happening. They all wanted to know, but none of them wanted to be the one to ask.

Albert started in their direction and was halfway there when he heard Melissa Medina call out from where she waited by her table.

"Why aren't we starting?" Her voice was loud enough that everyone in the marquee heard it. Competitors, judges, and factory staff alike all fell silent. "Who's in charge this year?" Melissa demanded, her eyes boring holes in the three people in their smart office wear. "Where's Mr Walsh? He should be here to start the contest, should he not?"

The trio, with all eyes on them, turned to face her, whereupon the two men promptly took a step backward to leave their female colleague facing the mob alone.

"Bella is in charge," volunteered the man on the left, getting a pat on the back from his friend who clearly thought stitching up Bella was highly entertaining.

She snapped her head around to glare at the men, who smiled sweetly and made hand gestures of encouragement. Prompted by more questions from the crowd of eager cooks, Bella tried her best to placate them.

"Um," she stuttered.

"Speak up!" insisted Melissa before the poor woman could even form a sentence.

Her cheeks were glowing, but Bella managed to say, "Mr Walsh cannot be found. Mr Barrowman will take over."

"So where is he?" demanded Melissa. It was a good question, to be fair.

Bella twisted around at the waist, hissing something at the two men behind her. They made apologetic faces and hurried from the marquee.

"My colleagues are attempting to locate him now," Bella did her best to remain in control. Addressing the entire audience, she said, "I'm terribly sorry for the minor delay, ladies and gentlemen. I think we can be certain Mr Walsh has been called to deal with a matter of extreme importance." The two clowns she'd been with, Charlie and Tom, were always pranking her. Well sticking her with the drama of a missing CEO – his car had been seen blasting out of the carpark less than five minutes ago – would play right into her hands. The firm was always looking for junior managers to promote and were very aware that they had only one woman on the Board of Directors. That was where she was heading.

Feeling more confident now, she decided to give Mr Barrowman, the firm's number two man, a minute. If he hadn't appeared by then, she was going to take over and start the competition herself.

"Please, everyone, return to your tables. We will be starting on time at exactly five minutes to ten."

From her table, Melissa shouted, "It's already ten o'clock."

Bella glanced at her watch and grimaced when she saw the annoying, loud-mouthed woman was right. Indeed, she could now hear the bustle of the crowd coming through the gates. The staff manning the entrance had opened on time, undoubtedly unaware of the drama unfolding in the marquee.

Where had Mr Walsh gone in such a hurry? And why hadn't he said anything to anyone?

Visitors started to wander through the marquee's entrance and that was all the motivation Bella needed. Marching across to the microphone, she tapped it with a neatly manicured fingernail. The sound boomed out of the speakers set around the marquee, startling her and she gave a little jump.

Forcing the heat from her cheeks and flicking her tongue over her lips to wet them as she stared out at the ocean of faces looking her way. The reporter from the Eton Mail aimed his camera at her and with a start, she made sure to smile. Confidently. Drawing in a deep breath, she opened her mouth ...

"Thank you, Bella." Stanley Barrowman darted across the stage. He had no idea where Oliver Walsh had gone, but he hoped it was permanent. With only three years between their ages, Stanley was never going to get the top job unless Oliver chose to go somewhere else or steered the company toward failure. Neither seemed likely, but the man had been acting strangely for the last two days as they worked overtime to prepare for the open day, and now he had left the premises in his car and allegedly at great speed.

Forcing a disgruntled looking Bella to one side, Stanley Barrowman waved to the people coming through the marquee's entrance.

"Hello, everyone. We're running a little behind today," he said with a chuckle.

Albert had wandered back to his table and was half listening to what was being said. Mostly, he was looking around at his fellow contestants and wondering if they would notice when he watched them like a hawk and copied exactly what they were doing. He knew it didn't matter if he made an absolute mess of the puddings - it was why he had a back up plan hidden in his fridge, but he wanted to give it a good go all the same.

Glancing to his right, and doing so carefully because Melissa Medina wasn't the least bit friendly, his head snapped out a double take.

She wasn't there.

His eyes flared, the whites showing as he twisted and spun in place, standing on his tip toes and ducking to look around people as he tried to spot her.

She was nowhere in sight.

How the heck had she managed to vanish in the space of the last minute? It couldn't be much more than that since she had last spoken. Regardless of how it occurred, she had gone, and Albert's heart was racing again.

The man at the microphone was still talking, but Albert wasn't waiting for him to finish. Hurrying to the plump middle-aged woman at the table immediately behind Melissa's, he asked, "Did you see where she went?"

"Who?"

"The lady who was there!" Albert spoke a little louder than he should as he jerked his arm at the now unattended table a yard away. More than a dozen contestants in his vicinity aimed frowns his way. Quietly, he repeated, "The lady who was right in front of you. The one who kept calling out."

The plump woman made it obvious she was trying to listen to the announcer, but peering around Albert to see the man on the stage, she muttered grumpily, "I don't know. She got a message on her phone and went outside. It looked like she was upset or angry or something."

Albert cursed under his breath and headed for the marquee's entrance. This was exactly what he had feared. Exactly the scenario he had predicted. They couldn't take her in such a public setting so had found a way to lure her outside.

Moving as fast as his legs would carry him without his knees protesting, Albert slipped around the people still filing into the marquee to arrive back outside in the daylight.

The scene was vastly different from earlier; the stalls, food trucks, and novelty games to entertain the youngsters were all busy, and people were queuing for their turn. A steady stream of visitors flowed through the gates and there were more behind them still.

For Albert it meant there were too many people. He frantically searched the crowd, but of Melissa he could find no sign. Had they grabbed her the moment she exited the marquee? He could picture it happening – someone comes from behind with a needle loaded with a knockout drug, Melissa falls and is caught and they act like she has fainted and just needs some air.

He needed to get high ... no, he corrected himself. He needed to watch the gate. In the thirty seconds since he left the marquee, no one had gone out through it, and he doubted there was another open gate anywhere. To get away they would have to take her out through the only available exit. All he had to do was watch it.

However, the moment the thought crossed his mind and his gaze zeroed in on the factory's wrought iron gates, the tall man in the suit with the slick brown hair walked through them. Beside him was a shorter man.

Albert wanted to blink and rub at his eyes. He was struggling to believe them, but there was no doubt in his mind. He was looking at the pair of thugs from last night. Had they not been standing together, he might have never figured it out.

Taking a step to his left to hide behind a potted fern tree positioned just outside the marquee entrance, he stayed out of sight and continued to watch.

It was them all right, but if they were just arriving it meant they either weren't after Melissa or were yet to get her. Albert felt the loathsome woman's attitude might benefit from a little recreational kidnapping, but all he was interested in was catching the Gastrothief's men.

It was too early to make his move now, but he needed to be ready to leap when they grabbed their target and for that he needed Rex.

What Did you Learn Today?

"This is called a fire door or an emergency exit," Rex explained. "Try to open it."

Eric's eyebrows twitched as he looked from the older dog to the door. It looked solid, and though he couldn't turn a handle if he wanted to, this door didn't even have one. How was he supposed to open it? All it had was an odd bar arrangement in the centre, just about at Rex's head height.

Nevertheless, he said, "Okay, Dad," closed his mouth and tried to paw at it. Then he tried to shove it with the top of his skull. It refused to budge as he expected it might. Was he supposed to take a run up and charge it?

"Good," Rex stepped in front of the door, effectively pushing Eric to one side. "Are you watching?" He wanted to correct the pup regarding his parentage, but having done so a dozen times already, it felt futile.

Eric's eyes bugged from his head when Rex jumped up onto his back legs and lunged forward with his front paws out. The handle thing in the centre of the door depressed and the whole thing swung open.

"Wowwwwwwww!" Eric gasped. "That was amazing."

Padding through the opening, his nose high in the air, Rex said, "Remember to look for emergency doors if you ever need to get out of a building."

Seeing what his alpha was doing, Eric copied, sniffing deeply to get a good noseful of air. He held it, sorting through the various scents it carried. There was food, a delicious mix of flavours, the odour emanating from a trio of wheelie bins parked around the corner out of sight, plus smells from the factory with which he was already familiar. Overlapping all of that were the people, each carrying a scent so individual he could separate them out and store them for later consideration.

What Eric didn't get was why they were doing it.

"What are we sniffing for?" he asked, embarrassed to have to ask the question.

Rex opened his eyes.

"The people I chased last night are here. Their smell was in your human's office, but it was faint and had to be at least a day old. I confess I really don't know what it is that we are investigating, but I believe our best course of action right now is to find them."

"Should we find your human first?" Eric suggested. He was curious to see how it was that Rex worked with the old man. Rex made it sound like he'd been able to train his human to understand basic commands and perform certain tasks that assisted Rex when he was trying to solve a case. It was all so fantastic, Eric wanted to see it first-hand.

Setting off, Rex loped along with his nose half an inch off the ground.

"This is how you search," he explained, taking Eric with him as he used his nose to find Albert.

Snooping for Information

While the dogs were looking for Albert and Albert was following two people he believed to be the Gastrothief's agents, Jessica was carefully unlocking the door to the CEO's office. Thirty-six hours ago, she had tried to access the files she needed from her own terminal. The gateway was encrypted, obviously, but over the last few months she had carefully and slowly asked the right questions to find out where to obtain what she needed.

Under the guise of working overtime, she spent many, many hours working late into the night to explore the firm's data files, both on paper and electronically. The information had to be here somewhere. It had to be.

It wasn't though. She pored through the whole directory of files and there was nothing there. It didn't come as a huge surprise because of course they would want to keep it hidden.

Finally, her persistence had paid off, but only because she'd recruited Joseph. A single question, dropped innocently at the right moment when they 'accidentally' met at the coffee machine one day just a couple of weeks ago, had set the health and safety manager on a hunt to find out if she could be right.

He came back to her just a few days later, whispering that he needed to see her after work. Janet, one of the girls at the office, had seen them whispering, and gossiping like a schoolchild, had wanted to know if Jessica was sleeping with him. Joseph was twice her age and desperately overweight, still it provided a convenient cover for their clandestine meetings so she played coy and refused to answer, knowing Janet would take that as a 'yes'.

People had been nudging each other and looking at her judgementally ever since, but it was of no concern. Joseph was on a mission now to find the information, the hard evidence, and promised he wouldn't stop until he had because his job, his career, and his reputation were on the line. Not to mention that he would go to jail if it ever came out – he was the one signing the paperwork!

He assured her the records were locked behind an encrypted gateway that could only be accessed using a key – a code that would be known only to whoever was managing the illegal activity. Convinced it had to be the CEO, Jessica spent another ten days snooping around his office after hours. She checked his notebooks and his drawers finding nothing that looked remotely like what she wanted.

Forced to take ever greater risks, she swiped his phone one day but found nothing on that either. The break came when he left his suit jacket in the boardroom, and she found his wallet in it. Tucked inside a small pocket between the credit cards and cash, was an old, crinkled business card for a Chinese takeaway and on it a ten-digit code written in faded black ink.

There was nothing written next to it, but the presence of such an old card hidden deep in the folds of the man's wallet told her she had found what she needed.

Joseph took the code from her; it was safer for her to let him poke around, plus he would recognise the damning detail when he saw it. He was going to download what he found onto a portable file and with it she would blow the lid on the whole sordid business. Her employers in London had the clout and the contacts to make it headline news.

But Joseph hadn't told her he was going to go fishing for it the same night she handed it over. Now he was dead, and she didn't have the data. Using the same access code, she tried to find what she needed herself, but it didn't work for her. A warning flashed on her screen, telling her she was attempting to access sensitive data she was not cleared for.

What she needed was a hacker, she thought. But maybe ... maybe it was because the CEO's terminal was set up differently. Mr Walsh had vanished from the premises in a hurry less than fifteen minutes ago.

Jessica had no idea where he had gone or why, but if she was going to jump on his computer and get what she needed, there was never going to be a better chance.

Do it Yourself. Do it Right.

Percy Crumley jolted when the alert message flashed on his phone. In so doing, he knocked over his espresso cup, spilling its contents and the dark liquid spread across the surface of his marble kitchen counter to drip onto the floor. Not that he noticed.

In his life he'd had only a handful of alert messages, sent whenever someone attempted to access his encrypted data. His team of accountants, well paid, and unable to walk away because they knew what would happen if they ever tried to leave, knew to forward the alerts to him whenever they occurred.

A handful in a lifetime, all of them false alarms because the greedy idiots at each business entrusted with access to the data forgot to call the accountants to say they were going to use their access code. Now

170

he had three in a week, and they were all genuine attempts to access his sensitive data.

The first call he made was to the accountants. It was picked up halfway through its first ring.

"Is this real?" he barked.

"Yessir." Percy recognised the voice. It was Isaac, a skinny whelp of a man who had been in his employ for more than twenty years. "That information is less than a minute old."

Percy strung together an impressive list of curse words, turning the air in his house blue.

He hung up without another word and dialled another number.

Chrissy paused what she was doing to see who was calling, and with an angry sigh that she did her best to suppress, she thumbed the green button.

"Chrissy what on earth are you doing? Have you got that Fletcher woman yet?"

"No, Mr Crumley. We are heading to her office now to see if she is there. This is a large factory and there are a lot of potential witnesses here. We are going to use the paramedic ruse, but we have to locate her first."

Percy knew the paramedic ruse well enough and had employed it himself a few times in the past. You knock your target out, then call a pair of contractors who have an ambulance and all the gear to make it look like they are real paramedics. The victim can be taken from under the nose of dozens of witnesses, and no one ever suspects a thing. Better yet, if the witnesses are questioned later, all they remember is that paramedics came.

However, now was not the time to applaud Chrissy's methods.

"Well, someone just accessed the system again. Someone at that factory is in there attempting to poke around right now. Get your thumbs out of your backsides, find whoever it is, and break their arms."

The news lit a spark just as Percy intended it to. Chrissy mumbled an apology and a promise to find the culprit, but Percy wasn't really listening. Things had gone too far, and he blamed himself for relying on other people. His empire was built by doing it himself. That way it got done right.

His bathrobe hit the carpet and he opened his wardrobe doors. He was supposed to be dealing with Oliver Walsh, but the man refused to return his calls. Walsh would get his later; he was a minor problem. Significantly higher on the priority list was plugging the hole at Wallace's.

Percy Crumley had already made his accountants empty the files. They wiped it all last night, but the problem persisted because someone knew something, and Percy needed to know who knew what. It was a hole in his ship, and he did not feel like sinking.

Not today. Not ever.

Right all Along

Albert had been tailing the Gastrothief's agents for ten minutes, following them from a distance and able to do so because the man was taller than everyone else. Also, the tall man was in a suit. It looked out of place at the open day and made him even easier to spot. In fact, Albert mused, he looked like he worked here and was a member of senior management or something. Perhaps that was his ruse.

The second man, the shorter one, was wearing jeans, work boots, and a dirty coat. All he needed to complete the picture of a person taking a break from working on a construction site was a hi-vis vest and a hard hat.

The two of them ignored the stands and stalls at Wallace's open day and walked right by the queue forming for the next factory tour. They were looking for someone, that much was clear, and they hadn't found them yet.

Again, it made Albert question his assumptions. The Eton Mess contest was happening without him, not that it mattered; he was here to catch these two in the act, nothing more.

They went into the marquee, a dead end with only one entrance or exit, so Albert hovered near the door, looking over the heads of the crowd inside. It meant he was able to confirm Melissa hadn't returned. The other chefs were busily whipping and fiddling, cutting fruit, or doing something Albert couldn't identify.

Was Melissa waiting somewhere for them to arrive? He didn't think so. Not anymore. If they had been the ones to lure her from the marquee, they would know where to find her, not be wandering everywhere trying to spot someone.

Albert was too far away to hear Chrissy's phone ring, but he saw the pair stop and then the phone appeared in the shorter man's hand.

Whatever the phone call had been, it got them moving. Before the shorter man had even put the phone away, they were hustling across the wide courtyard and heading straight for the factory itself - not the doors where the visitors taking a factory tour were going in, but a side door to the left in the shade of the building.

Falling behind as they moved faster than he could, Albert's heart caught when he spotted what they were heading for.

Melissa was ahead of them.

He'd been right all along. His knowledge of the Gastrothief and how his agents operated had steered Albert on a true course.

Melissa had a phone pressed to her left ear and was gesticulating wildly with her right. She was a yard or so from the factory, tucked away from the crowds behind the stalls touting their wares. There she could conduct her phone call in as much privacy as possible.

She had no idea of the danger coming her way!

Missing Data

J essica's frown was pinching her eyebrows together. The code
worked. She navigated to the files she wanted, attempted to open
them, and was prompted to enter the code. She'd first got this far
nearly a month ago, but didn't have the code. Then yesterday, even
with the code, she got into the system, but the files wouldn't open.

This time, with the code in her possession, she not only satisfied the
security check, but also managed to finally access the files. However,
instead of finding what she hoped would make her a hero in the eyes
of her organisation, and more importantly enable them to shut down
a dangerous and illegal activity, she found nothing.

Nothing at all.

The files were all empty.

"How can they be empty?" she voiced her confusion to the empty air and fought against the bitter disappointment crushing her will.

She was out of time, that was the biggest problem. That someone had come after her, that someone had killed Joseph, whether accidentally or not, was completely out of place with the nature of her investigation.

Sure, people would want to keep it hidden, but she didn't expect anyone to kill for it.

Telling herself she must have done something wrong, Jessica backed out of the files and started again. Just as before, when she clicked on the file she wanted, a box opened in the centre of the screen demanding she enter the security password.

Again, she accessed the files hidden behind the ten-digit security code, and just as before they were empty. She felt a desperate desire to throw something. Months of pretending to be someone else, and for what?

Movement in her peripheral vision, twitched her head around. The chief executive's office had a large window looking out over the factory floor. Heather Roberts, one of the team leaders from the warehouse was leading a tour of about twenty visitors through the factory.

They were just passing the boxing machine and like a surge of electricity, a question exploded at the front of Jessica's brain.

Joseph had taken her portable data storage device with the plan to copy the files when he accessed them. Jessica assumed he had achieved at least the first part of that which meant he had almost certainly copied the files as planned.

So where was her data storage device?

Straining her mind to find an answer, her nails dug into the arms of the CEO's office chair.

If Joseph copied the files, where was the data drive?

No, that was the wrong question, she decided. The files had been wiped, but if Joseph copied them, then they still existed, so the real question was, had 'they' taken it from him, or had he stashed it somewhere?

Biting her lip, Jessica carefully shutdown Mr Walsh's computer, made sure everything was as it should be, and locked the door to his office.

It was an absolute longshot, but Jessica felt convinced that the only reason Joseph had gone up into the elevated walkways was because he was being chased. Otherwise, he would have taken the information and left.

Was he pushed into the boxing machine, or did he fall? The police had confirmed there was no sign of foul play, and the access gate he fell through was found to be faulty. To the best of her knowledge, there was no portable data storage device found on his body, so if he did fall, and the people chasing him didn't get it, then it had to be up in the walkways somewhere.

The dogs had been alone in her office for almost an hour now. It was less than ideal, but finding those files was far more important and if Eric made a mess, well, it wouldn't be her office tomorrow. Turning left out of the chief executive's office, she avoided going anywhere near her own, certain the dogs would get excited if they saw her.

Wrong about Everything

Albert's heart raced as he tried to close the distance between him and the Gastrothief's agents. They were five yards from Melissa now and there was nothing he could do to prevent their attack.

He tried shouting a warning, but the sound of his voice was lost among the music playing, announcements coming over the public address system, and the general hubbub of conversation contained and amplified by the walls of the courtyard.

Hampered by a trio of mothers pushing toddlers in buggies, Albert had to stamp on the brakes to avoid piling into them as they moved to block his path unexpectedly. He caught glares from two of them and found himself automatically nodding his head in apology.

The gap between the couple and their target had closed to nothing in the two seconds he was delayed. There was no way to stop what was about to happen, but he could make enough noise that others would see the Gastrothief's agents taking Melissa.

It wasn't how he wanted to do things; there was too much chance that someone would get hurt. However, with no choice, and with no time remaining, he filled his lungs to bellow at the people around him, and grabbed the sleeve of a burly looking man to his right.

The yell of alarm froze in his mouth.

"Are you okay?" enquired the man whose sleeve Albert now gripped.

Albert couldn't tear his eyes away from what he was seeing. He could hear the people talking; they were asking him questions, but he had no answers for them.

"What's going on, Nick?" asked the burly man's girlfriend.

Nick removed Albert's unresisting hand from the sleeve of his coat, but kept hold of his arm.

"I don't know. I think he might be having a stroke or a seizure or something."

Albert's mouth was hanging open, and questions were filling his brain. The Gastrothief's agents had walked right past Melissa without giving her a second glance. Two seconds later, the large man in the suit produced a key from a pocket and opened the factory door.

A small crowd was gathering around him, but Albert needed to figure out what he was seeing.

Jessica was adamant that she didn't know who the couple were, yet they had keys to at least one factory door. Surely, that meant they worked here. But then why had they been following Jessica last night?

It wasn't the only thing that didn't add up. Earlier Jessica had thanked him for helping her and said carrying his shopping was the least she could do. When he questioned her, she brushed it off, but there was more. Last night, she had seemed too dizzy to walk home by herself. She never actually asked him to help, but once they were in her house, the concussion symptoms evaporated. Then the man checking in the contestants had been confused about why Jessica was here today.

Hands on his coat were trying to lower him to the ground and seeing the door swung shut behind the couple as they went inside, Albert fought to get free.

A woman wearing a thick jumper beneath a winter coat stepped in front of Albert's face.

"Sir, you are having an episode," she spoke loud and slowly. "Can you tell us what medication you are taking?"

"I'm fine. I'm fine. I'm not having a stroke," he argued. "Please, I need to go."

A voice Albert recognised filled the air, speaking louder than anyone else.

"Make way, make way." Edwina parted the crowd. "I'm his wife, let me through."

Albert's eyes bugged out and he almost spat, 'No, you are not!' but held his tongue because he understood what she was doing and the concerned people pressing in around him were already beginning to dissipate.

Playing along, he said, "Thank you, Edwina."

"He's always wandering off," Edwina quipped to those still in earshot. Then lowering her voice, she said, "Don't panic," and planted a kiss directly on his lips.

Panic wasn't the first emotion that sprang to mind, but he was hasty to take a step back and had to fight hard not to use a coat sleeve to wipe his mouth.

"I have to go," he blurted, hurrying toward the factory. Had they locked the door after they went inside? Would he have to find another way in? Whatever he thought was going on in Eton, it was something completely different and now he couldn't work out what his next move ought to be.

One thought was that he ought to be grabbing Rex and running straight for the train station. If he was wrong about this being a Gastrothief target, then his need to get to Cornwall had just grown exponentially. However, the fact that they were not after Melissa placed Jessica in danger and even though he now believed she'd been lying to him from the very start, in all good conscience, he still couldn't walk away until he knew she was going to be safe.

Racing for the door, a few words from Edwina stopped Albert dead in his tracks.

Scents that you Just Can't Fight

Rex had found the scent of the people he chased last night and was following it. That was, however, distinctly easier said than done. It was like trying to find a person inside their own home – hard because their scent was everywhere. With Eric lolloping along by his side, Rex had recrossed his own path half a dozen times.

His hunt was further hampered by all the other smells around, plus a light breeze and the constant passage of humans. He did his best to explain it all.

"They've taken a circuitous route, that's for sure," he remarked, staring at the marquee. His human was in there, he believed, and maybe it was time to get the old man involved. It was embarrassing to not be

185

able to trace a scent to its source, but at the same time, he was operating in terrible conditions.

Turning his head to make sure Eric understood what he was saying, Rex discovered he was alone. He spun around, looking for the pup, but his young charge was nowhere in sight. A tinge of worry set in.

"Eric!" he barked loudly, scaring two small children waiting their turn on a child-sized merry-go-round. "Eric!"

"Shoo!" The children's mother wafted her hands to scare Rex away.

He ignored her, turning away to scan a different direction.

The mum, looking around for an owner to berate, found none, and didn't like that one bit.

While Rex put his nose to the ground, sniffing out Eric to find him rather than using his eyes, which was just plain stupid and something a human might try, the mum started asking those around her if they owned the giant German Shepherd dog.

There was no sign of the pup, and the circuitous route they had taken as they followed the elusive humans Rex had been unable to locate, created the exact same problem in finding Eric.

Rex huffed his frustration and drew in a fresh lungful of air to bark the pup's name again. It was in that deep breath of scent-laden air that the answer arrived.

His huff became a chuckle, and Rex set off at a jog.

Just as he guessed, Rex found Eric with two long candles of drool hanging from his jowls. He was standing, his body quivering with excitement as he stared, unable to avert his gaze, at the entire hog rotating on a giant spit.

"Smells good, doesn't it?" Rex remarked with a smile and a long sniff as he came to stand next to the pup.

Eric whimpered, "It's like the smell has a direct route to my brain. I can't get my feet to move."

Rex chuckled. They were a few yards from the hog roast, unable to get any closer due to the queue of people waiting to be served, but Rex didn't think that was necessarily a barrier.

Trotting past Eric, he gave the pup a nudge.

"Come on, pup. Let me show you how it's done."

On wobbly legs and walking sort of sideways so he didn't have to take his eyes off the rotating pig, Eric followed.

Rex led him around the back of the hog roast stand, all thoughts of his human and the people he'd been trying to find temporarily forgotten. He would have felt bad about abandoning his duty if the thought occurred to him, but the smell of juicy, succulent pork and crispy pig skin had permeated every part of his soul and there was nothing in his world now save for a need to eat.

Now out of sight in the area behind the row of traders, Rex knew there would be few people paying any attention to what they were doing.

The question in his head was whether the humans running the hog roast stand would willingly throw them some scraps, or if he was going to have to make a grab for what he could get.

He didn't get to find out because Eric could contain himself no longer.

"Must. Have. Meat!" Eric yipped, running for the back of the stall on his spring-loaded puppy legs.

Rex barked, "No!" but it was too late. The puppy zipped under the hem of canvass hanging from the stall's collapsible steel frame to leave just the tip of his tail poking out.

The gap was too low for Rex to easily follow, and he had to get on his belly to shove his head under next to the pup.

Eric had gone no further because there were feet right in front of his face. Three pairs of them as the stallholders, two women and a man, carved and served and took money. Attempting to get any closer would result in tripping someone or getting trampled.

Rex bit hold of Eric's collar and dragged him backward, sliding on his side to bring the pup back under the canvas.

"That's not the way," Rex whispered. "Follow me." There was always a better way. Sometimes the better way was harder. Not today though.

Rex led Eric to the side of the stall where a stand was set up for customers to add condiments to their hot pig-in-a-bun sandwiches.

Eric saw it first and tried to move so fast that he fell over.

Rex sniggered, "Don't worry, kid. It's not going anywhere."

On the ground around the table, next to the bin, and in fact all over the old stone tiles of the courtyard, there were dropped pieces of pork. Lots of them. What got Eric so excited was a whole sandwich someone had dropped.

Between them, they scoffed down every last morsel in sight and the stallholders said nothing because it was saving them a clean up job.

By the time there were no scraps of pork left to sniff out, Eric's belly was full, and Rex was prepared to admit that though he wanted more, he could no longer claim to be hungry.

Remembering what he was supposed to be doing, Rex got his nose back to the task of finding his human.

The Closing Net

Albert stared at the door. He felt an urgent need to get into the factory. Now believing he was completely wrong about who the couple were and what their intentions might be, he remained convinced they were up to no good.

However, he twitched in place, unable to chase after them because of Edwina's revelation. Grimacing because he knew he had no choice, Albert turned around to face her.

"Let me see."

Edwina dutifully handed over Albert's phone. It was already in her hand and extended towards him.

"He's been phoning for the last couple of hours," she said, as she watched to see how Albert would react. She'd already read the messages appearing one after the other on his phone and had unashamedly told Albert of the message they contained. "What's the deal with Chief Inspector Quinn then?" she inquired, watching Albert's eyes flick across the tiny screen.

Albert didn't answer, not straight away at least.

The messages were from Roy Hope back in Kent, explaining in urgent tones that the game was up, and Chief Inspector Quinn was already on his way to apprehend Albert in Eton.

Albert discovered he was huffing his breaths in and out, one after the other through his nose. His eyes were locked on the screen of his phone and his brain was working overtime. It hadn't taken Chief Inspector Quinn long to figure out how to find him. That was a problem. Albert had hoped for at least a few days if not perhaps weeks, but the senior police officer was more dogged than Albert had given him credit for.

The good news was that Chief Inspector Quinn was heading for the Dog and Duck bed and breakfast where he believed Albert had lodged last night. Quinn would have no idea where to look for him once he arrived there and discovered it to be a dead end.

That said, was it safe to delay his departure from Eton? The sensible and obvious next action was for him to grab Rex and hightail it to the nearest bus or train station. Or perhaps a better plan would be to grab a cab that would take him to the next town just in case Quinn's determination to apprehend him led him to put officers at the obvious transport hubs.

Whether Albert chose to hang around for a couple of hours to make sure that Jessica wasn't in danger, or left immediately, he still needed to go into the factory to find Rex. With that in mind, he slid his phone into an inside jacket pocket with a murmur of thanks to Edwina.

"You're welcome," she replied, eyeing him curiously. "You appear to have a tale to tell, Mr Smith."

Her direct question, voiced in an innocent manner, drew a small snort of laughter from Albert's nose.

"That is one way of putting it," he remarked, setting off towards the same factory door the couple had gone through not two minutes ago. He got no more than two paces before he changed his mind and levelled a questioning look directly at Edwina. "Is Jessica your granddaughter?"

Edwina's eyebrows rose in surprise. "Of course she is. Why ever would you ask such a question?"

"Because she's up to something, Edwina, and I should like to know what it is."

Without another word, he turned on his heels and marched promptly up to the factory door. The question of whether they had locked it behind them or not was answered when he turned the handle and pushed it open.

Now inside the factory, he could hear the echoing voices of a tour group. They were some distance from him and would be oblivious to his presence he felt certain.

Getting his bearings, Albert spotted the offices looking down over the factory floor and started in that direction just as Edwina came through the door behind him.

"What do you mean she's up to something?" Edwina wanted to know, hurrying along behind Albert as he in turn pushed the pace to get to his destination.

Jessica had claimed she would be in her office and though he was a little discombobulated and unsure exactly how to get to it having come through a different door, he was also certain that he would find it if he persisted. In fact, the only question in his mind was who he would run into first? Members of factory staff who would question his presence and intentions wandering around the factory as he was, or the two men from last night?

A Glimpse at the Truth

Edwina continued to pester Albert with questions all the way up to Jessica's office, but Albert didn't have any answers for her. What did he think her granddaughter was up to? He didn't have a clue. Jessica had exaggerated her need to be here today and clearly had her own agenda for wanting him to come along.

Volunteering to help him get into the contest, selling him on the idea that she was acting altruistically because it was the right thing to do ... that wasn't it at all. No, she was caught up in something, and now he needed to know what it was.

Despite the virtual inquest, Edwina's presence proved helpful because she knew how to get to Jessica's office.

"I used to work here years ago," Edwina supplied an explanation for her familiarity before Albert felt the need to ask. "That was back in the early seventies," she continued. "I stopped working when the kids came along, but my Harry, he worked here until he was forced to retire. Not by the firm, you understand, he just got too old for it. His eyesight was going, and his knees ached all day long. I used to have to put bags of frozen peas on them when he got home at night. I wrote labels on them, left and right," she reminisced. "Funny the things you forget about until something calls the memory to mind. Well anyway, Harry bought into their pension fund, and it's been ever so good to me. It transferred over when he died, and it's kept the debt collector away from my door I don't mind saying. Oh."

Albert was half listening, following a step behind her as she led him through the building and wishing she would pick up the pace. He couldn't voice his desire though because his guide was older than he was and though sprightly, neither of them would be winning any races any time soon.

Her unexpected silence brought his attention back into focus to realise they had arrived. Jessica's office was right in front of him, but she wasn't in it, and neither was Rex.

"Well, where's she gone then?" Edwina muttered.

Peering through the window, Albert couldn't see the puppy either, though oddly Delilah was there. Spotting her human, Eric's mum had clambered to her feet and was wagging her tail, pleased to see someone she knew.

Albert heard Edwina open the office door and cooing noises from Edwina as she greeted her dog, but his attention was elsewhere. Through the glass walls he could see out to the factory floor where a lone figure in office wear was high up in the steel walkways where she had no right to be.

It was the splash of colour from her dress that made her so easy to spot.

So far as Albert was concerned, Jessica's presence up on the walkway ended any final doubt that she wasn't somehow involved in what happened to her dead colleague.

Rounding on Edwina, he grabbed both her shoulders to ensure he had every bit of her attention, and she would see how serious he was. Unfortunately, Albert forgot about a German Shepherd's in-built need to protect their human from any and all threats.

The dangerous growl emanating from deep inside Delilah's chest was enough to make Albert adjust his stance. Dropping his arms and stepping back, he nevertheless persisted with what he had to say.

"Edwina, you have to tell me what Jessica is doing here today. Why was she in Kent yesterday? Why are there people following her?"

Edwina's face contained nothing but mystery. If she was bluffing, she was doing a good job of it. With a shrug, she attempted to answer one of Albert's many questions.

"Jessica said she needed to visit her previous employers. That's why she went to Kent."

"Previous employers?" It was information, but not in the least bit informative.

"Yes, Jessica used to work for a newspaper. That was in London though. I'm not sure why she had to go to Kent, but it was definitely something to do with her job. Maybe she's trying to get it back."

Blinking, Albert pressed on. "What was her job, Edwina? What did she do at the newspaper?" He had a dozen more questions starting with what newspaper it was and why she quit, but they were going to have to wait. His feet were already itching with the need to catch up to her on the raised walkways. He wanted to confront her right where she was, engaged in whatever it was that she was secretly doing.

He expected Jessica's gran to reveal that the job was copywriter, or advertising executive, so the reply he got came as a shock.

"Investigative journalist. She was quite good at it, I was led to believe. I couldn't work out why she chose to work here as someone's assistant instead. It must have been quite the pay drop."

Albert reeled. Under any other circumstances, a big piece of the puzzle might have dropped into place, but today the nature of Jessica's former employment just added confusion.

Investigative journalist. The words echoed in Albert's head. Just like the guys who exposed President Nixon's Watergate scandal. Just like dozens of others who claimed huge scalps by exposing massive conspiracies or cover ups.

Like a surge of electricity hitting his veins, Albert saw through the lie. Jessica hadn't quit her job working for the newspaper, she was here undercover! What in God's name had he stumbled into this time?

With a determined snort much akin to a bull before it charges, Albert set off.

"Hey, where are you going?" Edwina called out as he left her behind.

Over his shoulder, Albert shouted, "I'm going to find out what is going on." Then to himself, he muttered, "Then I'm going to find Rex and get the hell out of Dodge."

The Grinch

Less than half a mile from the factory, the Dog and Duck B&B was playing host to some unwelcome visitors.

"I can assure you, madam," Chief Inspector Quinn sneered down his nose at the owner, "Albert Smith stayed here last night. He is most likely travelling under a false name. His reservation was made using a credit card owned by Roy Hope."

"Ah, yes," Camilla Clarendon smiled up into the face of the intrusive and overbearing police officer. "We had a reservation for Roy Hope."

Quinn turned to exchange a knowing and victorious glance with his driver, a young police constable called Wainwright. Wainwright was the unfortunate fool saddled with the task of ferrying the boss across the country purely by dint of not being quick enough to think up an excuse.

When urgent whispers in the locker room warned that the chief inspector was inbound, most of the other guys legged it, but Wainwright, unable to get his clothes on fast enough at the start of his shift – running late as usual – found himself shackled for the day.

They were miles from their constabulary, and to his knowledge the chief inspector hadn't told anyone in the area that he was here. It seemed Chief Inspector Quinn intended to arrest Albert Smith and cart him back to Kent for processing. It was unorthodox, but Wainwright wasn't going to pass comment.

However, the chief inspector's satisfied grin faltered when Mrs Clarendon added, "He never checked in."

"What?"

"Just as I said," Camilla tried to hide her smirk. "He never checked in. The room was paid for in advance for one night," she added with a shrug. "If they choose to not turn up, what business is that of mine."

The chief inspector's face had turned deep red, and Wainwright chose to back away a pace.

"A tall man with a bald head. He's in his seventies," Quinn persisted, unwilling to be beaten. "He must have booked in under another name."

"Not unless he somehow managed to also lose forty years and transform into a woman," Camilla replied, this time not bothering to hide her glee. The man demanding answers from her was perhaps the most loathsome police officer she had ever met. Not that she liked the police as a rule anyway. Her only experiences with them had been negative: pulling her over because she was going just a few miles over the speed limit (ok thirty, but what difference does it make?), rudely telling her to move along just because she wanted to see the aftermath of a serious accident. They were no fun at all. "We only had two guests last night and they were both single ladies staying in rooms by themselves." She swivelled her computer screen around to show the chief inspector. "See for yourself."

Challenged directly, Ian Quinn knew he was losing face in front of one of his youngest and most junior subordinates. He could continue to fight, but instead chose to issue a quiet warning.

Bending forward at the waist so his head came down to invade the space in front of Camilla's face, he said, "I am going to catch Albert Smith, and when I do, I shall find out if he stayed here or not. If you are lying, you will serve time at Her Majesty's pleasure, I can assure you. Aiding and abetting a known criminal is a serious offense."

Horrified, even though she was entirely innocent, Camilla nevertheless gasped and put a hand to her chest.

Now with the upper hand and shrewd enough to know when to quit, Quinn promptly about-faced and walked back out to the street.

"What now, Sir?" asked Wainwright, praying the answer was to return to their base in Maidstone.

Narrowing his eyes and staring into the distance, Quinn murmured, "He's here. That daft old man is clever enough to lay a false trail, knowing I would be watching his accomplice, Wing Commander Hope. But he's not as clever as he thinks. His double bluff, bringing me here just so I would think he isn't, is about to backfire. He's here, and his need to toy with me will be his undoing."

Wainwright thought that all sounded like a load of absolute guff, but he said, "Yes, Sir," and waited to be given an instruction.

Two minutes later, Ian Quinn was talking to Graham Murdo, an old pal from the police academy where they both trained, and calling in an overdue favour. Plainclothes officers were to be deployed to all the local transport hubs. The old man couldn't drive and had been travelling the country by train and bus for months. On top of that, they were going to start the process of contacting every B&B and hotel in a five-mile radius.

An old man travelling with only a giant German Shepherd as his companion. He wouldn't be hard to find.

It took every fibre of Ian Quinn's being not to grin like the grinch at Christmas.

Canine Subterfuge

Rex had followed the intertwined scents of his human, Eric's older human, and the couple he chased last night all the way to the factory door. It was closed and there was nothing he could do to open it.

"Do we find a fire door," Eric asked.

"Ah," Rex found himself at another teachable moment. "They only work from the inside. I believe the point is to escape if there is a fire inside the building. Humans see buildings as dens, and they only let in those they see as family or potential mates." Rex considered for a moment how those rules extended to friends as his own human often had male friends come to visit. Dismissing it as likely to add confusion instead of clarity, he finished with, "So they don't want people to be able to get into buildings unless they are welcome. Does that make sense?"

Eric's tail went still. "Not even slightly."

"Good." Rex rolled his eyes. "Well, either way, we need to find a different way in."

The problem with that was that there were humans everywhere and Rex knew well enough that dogs roaming by themselves were generally frowned upon. Remembering how the mom reacted when he barked and scared her two children, he needed a cunning plan if he was to get in through the big entrance he'd seen earlier.

Rex led Eric around the back of the stalls, going back to fetch him three times when the pup got distracted by a crisp packet blowing along the ground on the breeze, when he caught a whiff of a pie stand when they passed it, and when he stopped to poop.

Hurrying the pup along, Rex said, "We are going to try something, but you must stick close by my side and stay quiet. Can you manage that?"

"Yes, Dad."

Automatically, Rex said, "I am not your dad."

"Yes, Dad," Eric wagged his tail.

With another eye roll, Rex slipped around the final stall and peered out.

"Ready?"

"Yes, Dad."

Rex timed his move, calculating speed and distance, then nudged Eric into motion and scampered out to join the back of a line of humans being led into the factory.

"Just act like we are with the people in front of us," Rex hissed. "Don't get too close though. We don't want them to notice we are right behind them."

The file of humans walked through the main entrance doors and onto the factory floor being led by another human who was speaking loudly to make herself heard over the noise of the factory machines.

"Excuse me. Sorry. You can't bring your dogs in here." Bella was back inside the factory and helping out in any way she could to impress Mr Barrowman. Maybe Mr Walsh was gone for good; Mr Barrowman was certainly acting as if that were the case. She doubted it, but just in case she was hanging around and working when she could legitimately have already knocked off for the day.

Charlie and Tom had already gone home, but she believed this was the key to her impending success. They were making it easy for her – all she had to do was look better than those two layabout idiots and she would be their boss before they knew what had happened.

Spotting the last couple in line sneaking in with their dogs in tow – some people! - she hurried across the factory to politely expel them. She would act like the senior manager she intended to soon be and tear a strip off the guide once the tour was finished.

"Sorry. Excuse me," she called again because the couple were so brazen they hadn't even bothered to look her way. "Your dogs. You can't bring them in here."

Now close enough for one of the couple, the man as it happened, to look her way, she raised her eyebrows in what she believed to be a challenge, '*are you seriously pretending that you can't hear me?*'.

"Can I help you?" he asked.

Bella suppressed her desire to say what she wanted and went with, "I'm terribly sorry. This is a food preparation area, hence the hats and little booties you are now wearing," she used both hands to point to her own head and feet in turn. "Your dogs will have to wait outside if you want to take the factory tour."

"What dogs?" enquired the man's partner.

Bella, unable to believe they could stand there and just deny it, shot an arm at the space the dogs had occupied just a moment ago.

"But ..."

Rex peered between two pallets to be certain no one was following and got to see a woman in office wear scratching her head and calling out to attract the attention of someone else. The two humans she'd been talking to had hurried away to catch up with their party, leaving her looking confused.

"We might have people looking for us soon," Rex whispered. Turning around with a sinking feeling because he'd taken his eyes off the pup, Rex grumbled several obscenities and started running.

He believed his human was in here and could now also faintly smell both of Eric's humans. Overlapping them was the smell of the couple he chased. They were all in here somewhere. Finding them though, that was going to be a challenge.

He found Eric before he'd gone very far. The pup had his nose to the floor and was snuffling along like a search dog. Surprising himself, Rex felt his chest swell with pride.

"That's it," he encouraged, lowering his snout to do the same. "Search a grid pattern if you must and look for pockets where air gets trapped. Scents can stay there much longer than in an open space. Otherwise, you need to find where the human you are tracking has made contact with something. Those are the strongest markers and the ones that can be most trusted."

Eric yipped excitedly, causing Rex to insistently shush him.

More quietly, the pup whispered, "I found it. I've found my humans' scents."

Deferring to Eric, Rex encouraged, "Then lead me to them. You can do it." He had found the scent more than a minute earlier, but he was well practiced and knew all the tricks. The scents Eric recognised were intermingled with Rex's human and the questionable couple. Giving the pup a chance, Rex held back and let Eric lead.

What it's all About

At the ladder that led up to the walkway, Albert expected to perform the same dance as last time, but Edwina had no intention of going first.

"I'll just stand here and wait," she said. "You go on. It's not like Delilah can climb a ladder."

Albert accepted her response without comment, secretly relieved not because he felt climbing ladders and wandering around on elevated walkways where someone recently fell to their death, was a poor plan for a lady in her eighties. The relief came because he was glad he didn't have to voice what he knew would be an unpopular opinion. Who was he to judge what a mature woman was or was not capable of?

However, as he started to climb, looking up for his next handhold, he heard Edwina cackle, "Besides, I can get a good look at your bum from here."

Albert froze, but only for a moment before pressing on. Maybe she was teasing him, maybe she was serious. He had no wish to find out which it was.

At the top of the ladder, he emerged onto the steel mesh walkway and started along it. Jessica was fifty yards away, crouching to get close to the raised floor and ducking her head this way and that as she continued to look for something.

The noise in the factory made it easy for him to sneak up on her, and despite calling out, he got within a few feet before she twitched in startlement at his unexpected presence.

"Hello," he said in a tone that made it a challenge. "Looking for something?"

Jessica, red filling her cheeks, rose to her feet and prepared to deliver a lie. She'd concocted it in case anyone saw her in a location where she had no right or reason to be, but Albert cut her off.

"What's the case?" he asked, watching her face, and seeing the surprise form on her brow. "Industrial espionage? Illegally importing milk from Venezuela to avoid paying duty? Hoarding the strawberry supply and putting the Wimbledon tennis championships in danger?"

Albert's flippant questions told Jessica that her lies were pointless, so she went for the truth.

"No, Albert, something a little more serious. Toxic waste dumping."

Albert had no idea what she was going to say, but was glad to be right that she was working undercover.

Jessica continued, "There are teams of environmentalists monitoring the water in the Thames. It took them decades to get it clean again; a concerted effort from the seventies that saw species returning to the river that had been absent since the eighteen hundreds. A few years ago, a new decline began. Fish numbers were dropping, some invertebrate species vanished almost overnight. I was contacted two years ago by a woman I went to school with. I had no idea what she was up to now, but she'd seen my name in the paper after I helped to expose a scandal in parliament."

Albert had planned to accuse her of using him, demand to know where Rex was, and to then hoof it out of Eton without looking back. Now though, he was being drawn into her story and had nothing to say as he listened for what she might reveal next.

"The Environmental Agency tested the dead animals they found, and they contained levels of mercury, magnesium, rhodium, and palladium. There was more ... too many to list, in fact. Such a broad spectrum of minerals could come from any one of a thousand factories sited on the banks of the Thames, but anyone producing toxic waste is monitored and closely regulated. You know who isn't?

Albert supplied the obvious answer. "Wallace's."

"Among many others," Jessica added. "They are not monitored because they don't use any registered chemicals in their processes. It took me nearly two years to narrow down the list of suspects, and then months of trying to find a position here so I could investigate from the inside. I was lucky that the woman I replaced fell pregnant and took maternity leave."

"Coo, there's a good view from up here," said Edwina, appearing from a walkway to their right.

Jessica and Albert both swung their heads to look her way. The walkway met theirs at a right angle a few feet behind where Albert was standing, and they hadn't seen her coming because it passed behind a large hopper.

"Gran? How did you get up here?"

Edwina's eyes twinkled. "Young people think they know everything. I went around to the stairs on the other side of the factory. It's a longer route, but stairs are easier for Delilah."

Delilah's tail twitched at the sound of her name.

Albert wanted to get back to what Jessica had been saying; her visit to the walkway right by where Joseph died had to be in connection with the toxic dumping. Had he been undercover here too?

He didn't get to ask the question though, for he noted that Edwina's eyes were not focused on him, or on Jessica. Indeed, they appeared to be looking at a spot behind them both. Before he could question it or twist his head to see, Edwina spoke.

"Are these chaps with you?"

Albert spun around almost too fast for his legs to keep up and he grabbed a rail for support.

Approaching them, and holding guns in their right hands, were the two men from last night.

"Don't move," ordered Chrissy, the small calibre gun in her hand unwavering as she held it close to her body.

Hearing the short man's voice for the first time, Albert squinted. There was something about it, an odd quality that made Albert question what he was hearing. Had the man's voice not broken properly? Or was he much younger than Albert believed? He studied the short man's face, seeing a lack of stubble that made him question if he might be the taller man's son.

The gunperson's age was hardly pertinent though. The gun, however, was.

Both men were carrying Glock 19s; squat black guns made in Austria. Fitted with suppressors, which people more commonly called silencers, there was no chance anyone would hear them being fired over the noise of the factory.

"Back up," Chrissy commanded, jerking the gun at Jessica, then Albert. "You too, old man."

Able to understand the threatening behaviour, Delilah began to growl again, her hackles rising as her muscles tensed.

Chrissy cocked an eyebrow. "If the dog takes another step, I'll put a bullet between its eyes."

There was no sense that the threat would not be followed by action if they failed to comply.

Albert reached out to place an extra hand on Delilah's lead, doing what he could to make sure nothing unnecessary happened.

"I want the data drive Joseph Lawrence downloaded all the files to," Chrissy's voice was close to emotionless.

Jessica started to deny she knew anything about it, "I ..."

"Don't bother lying. Joseph ran when we cornered him. It wasn't on his body; we checked with the coroner."

"Yeah, he was most talkative when I started breaking his fingers," sniggered Kasper. He shut up again when Chrissy shot him a warning look.

Jessica was horrified by what she was hearing, but at the same time elated because she was right. Joseph had copied the files and if the bad guys were after the data drive, then her guess that he might have stashed it somewhere had to be right.

"We thought it was a dead end until you tried to access the same restricted files. The boss has a few questions for you, but first I think I'll take that data drive."

Stuttering, Jessica said, "I, I, I," then stopped, composed herself and looked her opponent straight in the eye. "I don't have it. I came up here to look for it. None of that matters though. Your whole organisation is about to crumble," she bluffed. "I already emailed my contacts at the Environmental Agency. This place will be swarming with inspectors by tomorrow morning. You can destroy the records that show when the toxins arrived and what was done with them, but they'll find the chemicals and trace them back to you." On a roll now, even though not one word of it was true, her vitriol continued, "There will be prison sentences for everyone involved ..." She had more to say, but the looks the pair holding the guns were exchanging made her words dry up.

"What on earth are you talking about?" Chrissy asked, her face scrunched with confusion. "Chemicals? Environmental Agency? This is about money, sweetie."

Speaking again, Kasper asked, "Do we shoot them here? No one will hear with the silencers on."

Double Ambush

C hrissy pulled out her phone and stole a glance at it so she could be sure to call the right number. Vlad and Niki were in the ambulance and on station waiting for her call less than ten minutes from the factory. The best solution was to knock everyone out – an unconscious form attracts a lot less questions than one with arterial blood pouring from it, plus lots of people can identify a bullet wound on sight.

However, instead of the one person they expected to have to deal with, they now had three plus a large dog.

There was probably no choice about shooting the dog and trying to cart out all three bodies was almost certainly impractical. Better to kill them here and leave their bodies to be found later.

The call connected before she could appraise Kasper of her decision.

"Yes," she replied to Vlad's question. "The factory main entrance. Come in slow, there's no need to draw too much attention. Kasper will carry her down to you unconscious." There was a pause as she listened. "Yes, just the one person for transport to Mr Crumley's residence."

Albert heard the subtext in Chrissy's words and prepared himself to act. That they were here for Jessica and intended to take only that which they came for meant they were about to shoot him and Edwina. Delilah too, he added mentally.

Shifting his hand slightly where it gripped Delilah's lead still, he intended to rip Edwina's hand away and send the dog on an intercept course. He wasn't happy about it, but if he could save just one of the ladies in the process, it would be worth it.

Albert had no expectation of making it out of the situation alive, so his actions were to be the last brave acts of a defiant man in the face of adversity.

He focused his thoughts, waiting for the right moment. He knew there would only be one chance and prayed someone would find Rex and make sure he was given a good home.

Chrissy never took her eyes off the trio, each of them silent now, though the old man had moved slightly. What was he doing? His hand had moved up the lead and he looked poised, his expression tense like he had a daft idea in his head and was about to set the dog free.

Bringing her aim down, she centred it on the dog once more.

Just when she was about to pull the trigger, she saw the old man's face change. A smile was forming.

His gaze had shifted too. He was looking behind her, trying to make her look no doubt. Well, she wasn't falling for that one.

Eric yipped.

The combination of suddenness and proximity made Chrissy jump. With her finger already on the trigger, all it needed was the twitch of muscle her spasm of terror induced.

The gun went off, scaring her again and driving a bolt of horror through Albert, Edwina, and Jessica.

Kasper jumped too, but he kept control of his weapon.

In the single second of silence that followed, both Kasper and Chrissy twisted to see the cute fluffball puppy wagging his tail obediently.

"My daddy said I was to sneak up on you and bark, but not until he was in position."

Had the humans understood what Eric said, they still wouldn't have been able to prevent what happened next.

Somewhere in his hindbrain, neurons fired, warning Kasper that he was in danger, and he turned to find his vision was filled with brown and black fur.

Rex's front paws hit Kasper just below his collar bones and while Rex bounced off, his limbs flailing as he tried to spot a landing on the walkway, Kasper careened backward into the railing.

Decades old, it stood firm, but it was never designed for people of his height and that meant the hitman flipped over the top. There was nothing beyond but free air and a long drop.

As Rex fell through the air, he was conscious that his human was shouting, but could spare no effort to decipher what the old man was saying. The steel mesh walkway was coming up fast and Rex knew landing was going to hurt no matter what he did.

A blur whizzed under his paws in the heartbeat before he slammed into the unforgiving grating, Rex's eyes tracking it to see Delilah rushing to aid Eric. The puppy had hold of Chrissy's trouser leg, and though his efforts were ineffective, Rex liked the kid's spirit.

Gritting his teeth as he readied to have the cold steel bite into his paws, Rex gasped in surprise when his human caught him. The old man couldn't control the load, awkward, heavy, and falling to earth as it was. However, the lurching stagger Albert managed before he spilled Rex to fall the remaining three feet to the walkway prevented the injuries he would surely have otherwise sustained.

"Golly, you need to go on a diet, boy," Albert heaved a huge breath and used the railing to keep himself upright.

Rex ignored the remark save to comment mentally that it was never going to happen and snapped his head around to go after the remaining hitman.

There was no one there.

Delilah and Eric had their heads poked through the railing, barking at their quarry who was hastily clambering down over the machine she'd landed on.

Chrissy saw what happened to Kasper, so when the old man released the dog he was holding, she vaulted over the side of the walkway. Unlike Kasper who fell headfirst all the way to the factory floor below, she dropped less than eight feet to land on the top of the churner. From there she vanished over the edge, dropped lightly to the floor, and ran.

Time to Rally

Percy Crumley handed over the pitiful five quid entry fee. It was all going to charity the lady on the gate assured him. Like he cared. Once inside, he patted his jacket, feeling the reassuring weight of the handgun under his left arm. Then he did the same for the one on the right, and after that went into a routine to confirm he had his knives, his blackjack, his knuckleduster and more.

Percy liked to be tooled up.

The factory courtyard was packed like he'd never seen it before. Of course, he'd only ever been here twice previously, he reminded himself and both those times were at night. Already in a foul mood due to Oliver Walsh's disappearance, Chrissy and Kasper's seeming inability to complete a simple task, and the general disruption to his finely tuned money laundering machine, he snarled and growled at anyone who dared to approach him and doubly so at those who got in his way.

Snatching out his phone with jerky, angry movements, Percy poked at the screen with his sausage sized digits, bringing up Chrissy's number.

She took her time answering, and when she did, the usual unflappable demeanour he'd grown used to was gone.

"Mr Crumley!" she blurted. "I think Kasper is dead. They ... one of the dogs ... I don't know how it happened. He never got a shot off!" she wailed.

"What? What do you mean Kasper is dead? How can he be dead? Pull yourself together. Where are you?"

"I'm ... I'm just leaving the factory. I had to look for another way out."

Percy barked a new order, "Turn around and go back into the factory. The job isn't finished."

"I can't do it by myself!"

"You won't have to. I am outside," he replied, speaking calmly. The situation was not how they might want it, but in his opinion, a person's ability is only truly tested when things go south. That's when they need to rally and find a solution. "If Kasper is dead, we need to make sure his body is taken away by our people, not by anyone else. Did you obtain the data drive?"

"No." Chrissy was doing her best to regain her control. Seeing Kasper fall had rattled her and only once she got clear of the factory had she stopped running. "No, Miss Fletcher claimed to not have it. She appeared to be looking for it herself. I think she was telling the truth."

"Well, I don't pay you to think," Percy growled into the phone. "I pay you to do. Where did you last see her and how long ago was that?"

Swallowing against the bile trying to rise, Chrissy managed, "She's not alone. That old man is with her again and there was an old lady too. Plus several dogs," she added as an afterthought. "They were on one of the raised walkways at the south end of the factory. That's where Kasper fell. It was less than a minute ago."

Patting the gun under his left arm again, Percy spat one more order. "Meet me inside."

Time to Call the Police. Or Not

H igh up on the raised walkway, utter bedlam had given way to disbelieving calm.

"You're sure you're okay, Gran?" Jessica had been convinced her gran must have a bullet hole in her. The bullet had gone somewhere, and it hadn't hit her or Albert.

Edwina hit her granddaughter with a disparaging look.

"I might be old, but I think I would know if I'd been shot."

Albert stood just a couple of feet away, one arm around Rex's shoulder as he thanked his dog for coming to the rescue.

"How did you ever get up there?" Albert asked, looking up at the roof of the hopper from which Rex had leapt.

Rex would have shrugged modestly if he could have, but licked his human's chin instead.

"Wasn't easy," he chose to admit. "Eric led us to you, and we saw the guns from right across the factory. I knew sneaking up on them from behind would be hard. So I found something to climb."

Albert looked into Rex's eyes for a long moment.

"I wish to God I knew what went on in that big brain of yours, dog." The comment earned him another lick on the chin and Albert rose to his feet as he wiped away the slobber.

Turning his attention to the body twenty feet below them, Albert knew the right course of action was to see if the man was dead, and if not, call for paramedics. Deciding he would get to that in a bit, he fired a question at Jessica.

"The short one said this was about money. Any idea what that means?"

Jessica, having accepted that her gran was unhurt, now questioned what she was supposed to do next. Call the police was an obvious move - someone had just pointed a gun at her. No, scratch that. Someone had just fired a gun at her and her gran and it was only blind luck one of them wasn't terribly injured or worse.

Being an investigative journalist was supposed to come with some tangible risk, but she was way beyond her comfort zone now.

To answer Albert, she said, "None whatsoever, but they wanted the data drive with the files Joseph downloaded. There must be something on it that we don't know about."

Edwina asked, "Like what?"

Neither Jessica nor Albert could supply an answer, but they all knew it was something worth killing for and it had to do with money.

"It might be drugs. Or drug money to be more precise," Albert hazarded a guess.

Jessica snarled at the air in frustration. "We need that data drive. I don't care about drug money or whatever else it might be. When I recruited Joseph to help me, he said there were discrepancies with the figures, that's how I convinced him to help me find the data. He said he had no idea why the paperwork recording the inflow and outflow of chemicals used in the factory – here they are mainly used for cleaning – were inaccessible. He said it ought to be public knowledge, that there was no reason for it to be any more secret than gran's weekly shopping list. That's why he agreed to help me find the data. It's what got him killed. I think we can assume Mr Walsh kept all the dirty dealing on one encrypted file. I guess he thought he was being clever."

Edwina asked, "So what do you do now?"

Jessica took out her phone. "Things have gotten way too dangerous. No one was ever supposed to get shot at. I'm calling the police.

Edwina reached out a bony hand and clamped it over her granddaughter's, preventing her from making the call.

"You can't," she said, her eyes locked on Albert's. "Can she?"

Albert sucked some air between his teeth and sighed.

"I'm not going to stop you, but if the police are coming, I need to go."

Jessica contorted her face to show she had no idea what was going on.

Albert explained as swiftly as he could. "You read about the explosion in Whitstable a couple of nights ago?"

"Cor, that was you?" Asked Edwina, sounding impressed.

"No," Albert choked, "but I was there pursuing the Gastrothief's agents, and the police believe I am involved now."

"Wait," Jessica shook her head to clear it. "You mean all that rubbish about the Gastrothief is real?"

Albert nodded his head in a weary manner. "Yup."

Jessica's mouth hung open as she revelled in the full extent of what that could mean, only shutting it when her grandmother nudged her arm.

"Perhaps we should get out of here," suggested Edwina.

Jessica made a frustrated face. "I still need that data drive."

"My data drive," boomed a loud voice from the factory floor.

The three dogs and the three humans all turned to look. On the factory floor twenty feet below them, a man in a sheepskin coat which he wore open to show the shirt and jumper beneath, looked up at them. Good at reading people after an entire career in the police, Albert knew the man was a career criminal just by looking at him.

"Do you know who this is?" Albert hissed from the corner of his mouth.

Rex sniffed the air, getting the man's scent. Eric copied him.

Jessica gave a short shake of her head. "I've got no idea."

Still whispering at a barely audible tone, Albert said, "Then I believe we can assume he works with the other two. We need to get somewhere public. Start to back away and let's see what he does."

What Percy Crumley very predictably did when he saw what they were doing, was rip the gun from under his left arm and start firing.

Unmistakable Sounds

"Did you hear that, Sir?" Constable Wainwright turned to look at the chief inspector, certain he'd just heard the staccato pop of low calibre handgun fire.

Quinn's face contorted into a sneer. "Albert Smith," he spat. It was a guess, of course, but he wanted whatever disturbance was occurring to be at Albert Smith's hands. It would justify all that he'd been saying and his demands that Albert's offspring all be suspended from active duty.

He almost ordered Wainwright to get in the car – they were parked around the corner from the B&B still, watching it on the off-chance Albert Smith might go back there. Quinn was certain the landlady had been lying.

However, the unmistakable sound of gunfire had stopped, and the echoes had faded away. He couldn't know where it had originated; all he had was a rough direction, so with his constable in tow, Chief Inspector Quinn set off to see if he couldn't locate the source.

What he really needed was for the gunman to fire a few more shots.

The Chase

"Chrissy!" Percy barked at his phone. It was a fruitless gesture since she hadn't picked up his call. He swore and stuffed the device back in his trouser pocket. Aiming his voice at the maze of walkways above him, he shouted, "I want the data drive. If you give it to me, I promise I won't hurt anyone."

Edwina fired back a rude word in response and Percy let off three more shots in the general direction he thought she might be.

The moment Percy went for his gun, Albert had yelled for everyone to leg it and with a shove got them moving. A shout over his shoulder ensured the dogs followed.

Quickly overtaking the humans, the dogs led the way.

Eric was loving every minute of it. Running alongside Rex, he barked, "This is great, Dad. Is this what it's like every day for you?"

Rex didn't get to answer because his human was shouting.

"Go right, Rex!"

Edwina was doing the steering and adamant about which way they needed to go if they wanted to get out. There was an exit at their level that led to an old fire escape. It would come out behind the marquee, she claimed and that was as good as they were going to get.

Another shot rang out, the bullet hitting the steelwork not a yard from Jessica's head. All three humans blurted colourful words and ducked. They had been doing okay so far because there was a lot of machinery and steelwork around them. Right ahead though, was a wide-open space at least three yards long. If the crazy man with the gun was waiting for them, they would be easy targets.

Seeing the humans hunkered down, Rex ran back to them. He intended to get them moving and was going to bark in their faces until they were back on their feet. Only just before he got to them, a scent caught his nose.

He was smelling Eric's human, the younger one, but not directly. The smell was coming from a crevice between two panels of a machine's outer casing.

He sniffed at it, confirming what he knew before pulling back to peer into the hole. There was something in it.

Seeing him, Edwina, Jessica, and Albert watched as Rex pawed at the crevice.

Jessica shot a glance at Albert.

"You don't think ..."

Albert nodded without having to think. "Yes, I do." He raised his head and looked about for the gunman. He hadn't gone, Albert didn't believe that for one moment, and the longer they stayed where they were, the more likely it was that he would find them.

In a crouching shuffle, he started moving again.

"What've you got, Rex?" Albert asked when he drew level with the dog.

Rex was getting frustrated by the thing in the crevice. He didn't really want it; it was neither food nor a toy, but the fact that it was eluding him was annoying.

Albert eased Rex to one side and reached a hand inside, withdrawing it a moment later with Jessica's missing data drive.

Her eyes lit up.

"I've got to get this to a computer! This could be everything we need." She came to her feet, turning around to head back to her office just as Percy's face appeared at the top of a ladder not twenty yards behind them.

Albert yelled, "Run!" and grabbed her arm to make her go the other way.

Percy saw the little black data drive in Jessica's hand as she took flight and screamed obscenities as he brought his gun above the level of the walkway. With only his head and now an arm above the ladder, he took aim.

Half a mile away, Chief Inspector Quinn corrected his direction of travel and increased his pace.

True to her word, Edwina found the exit on their level and the marquee was right outside. They spilled onto a galvanised steel landing outside. Albert found a rusting old length of chain which he used to secure the door handles. It might not hold the crazy gunman for long, but any seconds he could buy them were needed.

Albert was out of breath. So too were Jessica and Edwina, but there was no time to stop for a breather. Dashing down the stairs with the dogs leading the way yet again, they heard their pursuer reach the fire exit door and find it wouldn't open.

Reaching the ground, Jessica aimed an arm at the marquee.

"We can hide in there!" she managed between gasps of air.

Telling the World

Understanding the clear instruction without needing it to be repeated, Rex bounded forward taking Eric with him. Rex didn't fully understand how the attachment worked, but Eric had already picked him over his own mother, the only other dog in his life until yesterday.

The pup wanted to go everywhere Rex went and do everything Rex did. Delilah, much to his surprise was completely unbothered by the change in her pup's attitude. It was as if she was ready to see the back of him.

All the excitement of the last hour, combined with the closeness to a female in season had put Rex in the mood for a little intimacy. Hurrying for the marquee with Eric at his side, Rex swung his head to shoot Delilah a meaningful look – maybe they could schedule a little 'alone time' when all this was done.

However, his face clearly wasn't forming the expression he intended because Delilah's response was to roll her eyes and look away.

He was still looking at her and trying to look cool and attractive when he ran straight into the back of the marquee.

"Are you okay, Dad?" Eric asked, looking up at Rex and wagging his tail.

"Um, yeah, sure, kid," Rex mumbled as he used a front paw to rub at his face where he'd just smooshed it.

The humans arrived, Jessica getting there first on her younger legs. Behind them, the sound of someone slamming their body into the fire door at the top of the stairs kept them moving.

"Do you think it will hold? Jessica stared up at the door, expecting it to explode outward at any moment.

Albert risked a glance, but knew the safest thing they could do was get out of sight. Anything they did to delay that increased the risk of getting shot at again.

Joining Jessica in gripping the bottom edge of the marquee's canvas sidewall, Albert pulled upward to make a gap underneath. Sitting on the old flagstone tiles of the courtyard as it was, the marquee hadn't been pegged down and was relying on gravity to hold it in place.

They saw feet on the other side, all facing away from them and realised they were coming in behind a line of the Eton Mess competitors. No one was looking their way and they were able to all duck under the curtain of canvas without being spotted. Now fanned out in a line with the dogs in front, they felt some modicum of security from the proximity of other people, yet hanging around remained a poor option.

"I need a computer," Jessica muttered, mostly to herself. To see over the people in front, she was on her tip toes, and spotting something, she jumped in the air to get a better look.

Edwina wasn't looking for a computer, she was staring at all the fancy Eton Mess puddings on display. They were making her hungry and there were so many of them. Surely one or two wouldn't be missed.

The marquee was mostly silent save for the voice of Mr Barrowman who was once again the focus of attention as he wrapped up the pudding contest. Judges would shortly be coming around to taste and score all the puddings, he announced. Contestants were to wait with their puddings and may the best cook win.

Albert wasn't listening, he was trying to figure out whether they were best served trying to leave the premises or finding someplace to hide. He needed to get the ladies to safety and realistically that meant the police. It also meant he needed to get Rex, collect his bags and leave, but he couldn't do that until he knew the people with him were no longer in danger.

Also, it rankled him to walk away when he was clearly right in the centre of an important discovery. Three hitmen armed with guns and mention of an ambulance to take the intended kidnap victim away dictated that this was an organised group. The precise nature of their crime remained a mystery, but not for long if he could help it.

"I found one," Jessica called out, interrupting Mr Barrowman who was now droning on about the importance of taking part and how there were no real losers.

Albert heard a voice comment, "Everything but first place is losing." It wasn't meant to be heard by everyone, but Albert knew it had come from Melissa Medina before he spotted the loathsome woman behind her desk just a few yards away. The desk to the left of hers was empty and the only clean table in the whole marquee because it was his and he hadn't so much as cracked an egg.

Mr Barrowman heard Jessica's raised voice and shot a frown in her direction. Of course, by then she was weaving through the tables to get to the judges' dais.

Edwina was following her, keeping Delilah in check on her lead. Rex waited for Albert who chose to follow the ladies, and Eric tagged on next to his 'dad' as the six of them prepared to make a scene.

Emerging from the front row of contestants, hundred of eyes turned to look at the odd procession.

"Here, you can't have dogs in here!" exclaimed one of the contestants, her sentiments echoed by many others.

"Miss Fletcher what is the meaning of this?" Mr Barrowman demanded to know.

Ignoring him, Jessica kept going straight as an arrow for the one laptop she could see. It was open and attended by a man in his twenties – one of the judges' sons who had been roped in to helping very much against his will.

"I need to use that." She didn't frame it as a question.

"Miss Fletcher," Mr Barrowman was getting angry. He did not like being upstaged or interrupted.

"Is it connected to the internet?"

"What about the dogs?" shouted someone.

It was quickly followed by a cry from the mom whose kids Rex scared earlier. "That's the dog who attacked my children!" she wailed as if the placid German Shepherd with puppy in tow was a vicious beast to be driven from town by a mob.

The young man behind the desk looked up at the cute red head, pausing to admire her ample chest before he got to her face.

"Hey!" Jessica grabbed the laptop, spinning it around so it faced her. "Is this connected to the internet?" she demanded more urgently than before.

Startled by her behaviour, the young man blurted a reply. "Um, yes. Yes, I've been loading pictures for the town's social media profile."

Melissa Medina, seeing a chance to get rid of the old man who clearly had to be cheating (just as she suspected from the start) because he hadn't even been at his desk today to make an Eton Mess, shouted,

"Get those dogs out of here!" Encouraging those around her to join in, she shouted again, "Get those dogs out of here! Get those dogs out of here."

The chant quickly filled the marquee and as more voices joined it became loud enough to be heard outside where a man with a gun angled his feet toward the giant white tent.

Albert, very much the fifth wheel now, could see no option but to comply.

"I'd better do as they say," he said, holding his hand out for Edwina to give him Delilah's lead. "Will you need long?"

Jessica's hands were prancing across the laptop's keyboard. She gave a short shake of her head.

"No. A couple of minutes max. The long bit is waiting for the files to transfer."

Doing his best to ignore the chants, Albert began backing toward the marquee's doors.

"I'll be just outside."

With hurried footsteps and refusing to make eye contact with any of the disdainful expressions aimed in his direction, Albert led all three dogs from the competition area.

Mr Barrowman reached the end of his patience. "MISS FLETCHER! I expect to see you in my office on Monday morning to explain yourself.

Without looking up, she replied, "I quit," and slammed the data drive into a port on the laptop's side.

Edwina asked, "What are you doing, love?"

"Sending this to my friend at the Environmental Agency and to everyone at the newspaper." With a flourish, she clicked attach to a hastily typed email and hit the send button. "Whatever is on it, it's now out there in the world and no matter what happens to us there's nothing they can do to stop the truth from being known."

"Then you'd better hope it was worth the price," snarled Percy Crumley.

The Best Contest Ever

Jessica froze. For the last couple of minutes her attention had been on nothing but the laptop. Because of that, the crazy guy with the gun had snuck up on them with ease. The gun was not in his hand now nor anywhere in sight, but Jessica doubted it was lost.

Percy dearly wanted to just shoot the woman glaring insolently back at him. Had she really just sent the files showing his transactions to a newspaper? If she had, it was over for him and he would have to flee the country, change his name, and live on the run, both from the authorities who would want to put him in jail for a very long time, and from the various crime families whose money he was about to lose.

If he acted fast, he might be able to move some of it around to prevent the police seizing all of it, but whatever happened, he was going to take great pleasure killing Jessica Fletcher.

He'd almost left the factory grounds when he burst through the fire door to discover he'd taken too long, and his prey were nowhere in sight. However, the chants gave him hope that all was not yet lost. Coming into the marquee, Percy had enough presence of mind to put his gun away, but with rage firmly in the driving seat he no longer cared about witnesses.

The old man and the dogs were nowhere in sight, so he was going to shoot the old lady and wound Jessica. Chrissy said the ambulance was coming and that gave him a way to escape with Miss Fletcher. She might have sent his files to the world, but he was going to find out who she really worked for, who the old man was, and how close the authorities were to breaking down his door. Then he would kill her too.

"Sir, this area is for contestants only," Mr Barrowman, unused to such bedlam in his calm and organised world, was doing his best not to start shouting and swearing.

Percy jinked his head and eyes to the right to look at the man who had spoken.

Jessica was rooted to the spot, but Edwina wasn't, and seeing the opening she needed, seized the moment of distraction.

Two feet to her left was the nearest of the contestants' tables. In one swift motion, she scooped an Eton Mess in a large glass bowl and flung it at Percy Crumley's head.

He was still reaching for his gun, trying to decide whether he should shoot the man who had spoken to him as well. He hated people in suits. Hated people in managerial positions and always had. They always looked down on everyone else as if they were somehow better.

Shifting his gaze back to Jessica as he withdrew the gun and a ripple of gasps reverberated around the marquee, he never saw the Eton Mess coming.

It hit him full in his face just as he got his head pointing toward it.

The audience gave a collective, "Ooooh," as his head rocked back.

Edwina had expected the glass to smash and didn't really have a plan for what she was going to do next. However, she was grabbing for a second pudding already when she heard the first one smack into Percy's head like a baseball thrown at a wall.

The sound made her head twitch around in time to see the pudding bounce off his skull. It fell to the ground where the glass promptly did smash.

By then the contestant whose competition entry she'd just employed as a projectile weapon had reacted.

"Hey! What the heck?" Arthur Royal didn't hold out much hope of winning the contest, and didn't even particularly enjoy taking part, but his wife insisted he come along so she could show off to her 'friend' Mildred, that *they* were a couple who did things *together*.

She was right, they did, but only because she henpecked at him until he gave in and complied. Her table was next to his and through the whole contest she'd been nagging that he wasn't doing it right. His strawberries were cut too small, then they were cut too big. He was being too vigorous in whipping his cream ... the list was endless.

Percy wobbled back a pace, his head swimming from the blow. Not many people had spotted the gun in his hand yet; the onlookers were too absorbed by the bizarre antics unfolding on the stage - the old lady had thrown a pudding and was trying to get hold of another one now.

Arthur and Edwina both had hold of the same glass bowl, wrestling for it briefly until Arthur's superior strength won. He snatched it from her grasp, hugging it to his chest protectively.

"What the devil is going on?" he snapped, looking at the judges who appeared as shocked and frozen as everyone else.

Percy shook his head hoping that would clear it, but it just made his vision go fuzzy. Raising both hands to grab his head and hold it steady, the gun in his hand became visible to everyone.

Screams and shouts of, "He's got a gun!" and the beginning of a stampede for the exit ended abruptly when Edwina snatched the third of Arthur's puddings and sent it after the first – right into Percy's face.

With his hands already full, Arthur could do nothing to stop the deranged woman from destroying what was now half of his entries and hoped the judges would mark him leniently because none of this was his fault.

The glass bowl chose to smash on Percy's forehead, finishing the job the first one started. He hung limply for a second, before folding like a ragdoll into a pile on the ground. The last chunks of strawberry, cream, and meringue that had been sent skyward upon impact with his head, fell to earth, coating his unconscious face like a final insult.

Applause erupted, many of the audience behind the barrier assuming this was part of the show.

Arthur, however, knew that it wasn't.

"Someone arrest her!" he shouted. "Someone do something before she throws another one!"

His wife, who Arthur felt ought to be doing something to help, made a scoffing sound.

"Oh, do stop making a fuss, Artie. Yours are the worst puddings in here. It's no wonder she picked them to throw."

Afterward, Arthur would spend many hours trying to decide if it was her words, the mocking expression on her face when he looked at her, or the previous thirty-eight years of marriage, but something snapped deep in his head. Scooping a handful of the Eton Mess he held, he threw it at her face.

"Take that, you 'orrible old bag!"

Shocked, Mildred opened her mouth and consequently caught half of what he threw in it. The rest splattered her face and hair.

The crowd cheered again and chuckled, loving this year's staged antics. They weren't the only ones. More than a dozen contestants around Mildred burst out laughing.

Hopping mad now, and ready to use her kitchen knife to stab her husband, Mildred wiped the cream from her eyes to find Arthur had already legged it. Arthur knew only too well that Vesuvius was about to erupt and was getting out of Pompei while he could.

"Think it's funny, do you?" Mildred spat at the people around her while reaching for a handful of her own pudding. She threw it, and then another, and another, pelting anyone in reach with globs of Eton Mess.

Each time she hit someone – they were moving targets now ducking below their tables to evade the madwoman's aim – the crowd cheered and laughed.

Mr Barrowman, unable to believe his eyes, called out, "Madam, please. That's quite enough now."

Wheeling around, Mildred screeched. "Oh, you want some too!"

Mr Barrowman ducked, the handful of pudding flying harmlessly over his head where it struck the head judge, splattering on her crimson top to make it stick to her chest.

She screamed in her disgust.

Mildred wasn't done, but around her the contestants unwilling to abandon their own Eton Mess puddings for the judging was supposed to be starting, were reaching for someone else's to throw in defence.

From the audience, a teenage boy, dragged out by his mum and dad because they weren't daft enough to leave him at home alone, shouted, "Food fight!"

It was echoed by another voice, and for the second time in as many minutes, a chant broke out.

Of course, the food fight was already underway, spreading along the rows of tables as more and more contestants found there was no option other than to join in.

Mr Barrowman attempted to intervene, but slipped on a puddle of whipped cream to land painfully on his backside. Seeing him go down, Bella, back in the tent so she would be seen by the boss applauding and cheering like a good team player, grabbed a whole Eton Mess and threw it at the back of his head before merging with the crowd and playing innocent.

When the melee arrived at her end of the marquee, Melissa Medina squealed, "No! No! Not my puddings. These are the winning puddings!" She used her body to protect them, absorbing blow after blow as poorly aimed puddings or fragments thereof coated her arms, legs, back, and head.

The food fight lasted no more than thirty seconds, but in that time every single Eton Mess pudding was destroyed. All bar Melissa's. They survived because she picked up her lazy Susan and ran with it, evading the flying puddings as if she were in *The Matrix* to arrive in the centre of the marquee where she could see anyone should they attempt to get her.

Calm descended. Well, apart from the audience who were whooping and hollering their appreciation. It had been quite the spectacle.

Having avoided the Eton Mess massacre by hiding behind the judges' tables, Jessica peered out to see what had become of her gran.

Edwina, feeling devilish and knowing she had started it all, had chosen to join in. There were plenty of puddings to go around. Of course, she now looked like a walking Eton Mess. Jessica got to watch as her gran found a piece of cream covered meringue on her coat and popped it into her mouth.

On the ground, the mad gunman's left leg twitched, spurring Jessica into motion. She turned back to the young man whose laptop she highjacked.

"I need your belt," she insisted, holding out her hands for it.

"My belt?" he stammered.

When he blinked at her and didn't move, Jessica grabbed for it.

His chair toppled as he tried to get away. "Arrrgggg h!" the young man cried. "Sexual assault! Sexual assault!"

Grunting, "As if!" Jessica snatched at the buckle and yanked his belt free.

Edwina, one eyebrow hitched, asked, "What are you doing, Jess?"

Jessica took the belt to Percy's unconscious form.

Over one shoulder as she rolled him over and grabbed an arm, she said, "Tying him up. I know Albert doesn't want the police here, but you can hear the sirens, right?"

Edwina nodded. The police were coming, reacting to more than a dozen phone calls from local residents: they had all heard someone shooting at Wallace's factory.

With Percy's arms secured, Jessica kicked his gun away just to be sure.

"Gran can you watch him and make sure no one touches the gun?"

"Sure. What are you going to do?"

"I need to help Albert escape."

Eric's Moment

When Albert left the marquee, he intended to just hang around outside. Jessica sounded confident that she wouldn't need long. That was a good thing because all the shooting was bound to draw the police. It might not have been audible to the people in the factory because of the machine noise, and almost certainly hadn't reached the ears of those outside because the factory walls would contain it and there was a lot of sound in and around the courtyard. Nevertheless, Albert was willing to bet people two streets over had heard it.

Regardless of the likelihood of the authorities arriving, hanging around when there was a mad gunman after them was foolhardy to say the least.

He had Delilah on her lead, and Rex was being good; staying to heel as Albert requested which somehow meant the pup stayed too.

More than ever, Albert felt the need to be on his way.

Rex's heartrate had come back to normal after the excitement in the factory. Humans and their guns. He really wasn't a fan of guns. They made his ears hurt and he'd seen first hand the damage they could do.

His thoughts were of Delilah and his intention to 'rendezvous' with her later. Or now. Now would work for him. He turned his head to look her way, planning to say something cool when a scent caught his nose.

When Rex rose to his feet, his human warned, "Stay, Rex. Now is not the time to be running off."

Albert leaned over to hook a hand through Rex's collar.

Eric had smelled it too. "It's her, isn't it, Daddy?"

Rex looked down at Eric. "Yes, kid, it is."

Chrissy had made the decision to run – she had no idea where she was going, but with Kasper lying dead in the factory, it wasn't going to be long before the whole place was crawling with cops. Mr Crumley was going to get himself caught and she wanted no part of that. She had been in prison before and had no plan to ever go back.

Ducking out of sight on the far side of the factory, she stripped off her man clothes and donned a thin dress. It didn't really go with her boots, except in a nineties grunge band kind of way, but the point was to change her appearance. Assuming Mr Crumley didn't kill the woman and the old couple, they were going to give her description to the police. Well good luck with that.

With her coat back on, it wasn't warm enough to be out in just a dress and people would remember her if she stood out like that, she headed around the factory to join the crowd. She would head directly for the exit and would vanish, maybe leaving the area for a while.

Coming around the side of the marquee, she could see the factory gates just thirty yards away, but that was when the breeze carried her scent to the dogs' noses.

Pulling against his human's grip, Rex barked, "It's her! The one you wanted me to chase last night!"

Eric yipped, jumping up and down in his excitement. "Let's get her, Dad! Let's get her!"

"Calm down, Rex!" Albert dropped Delilah's lead and shifted his right foot to trap it, then used both hands to control his dog.

Rex barked, "Go, Eric! Get her for me, kid!"

The puppy yipped with excitement and bounded forward, his unsteady legs producing a lolloping run as he chased after Chrissy.

She was nearing the gate. There were sirens approaching; the police were less than a minute away, but that was fine. She would be long gone by then.

Five feet from the exit and without warning, her dress caught on something. Twisting at the waist, she looked around and down to find a German Shepherd puppy biting hold of her dress's bottom hem.

It was drawing the attention of those around her, the very thing she didn't want. Not only that, it was the same puppy that had surprised her up in the walkways right before the big dog attacked Kasper. If the puppy was here, the other dogs couldn't be far away.

Back at the marquee, Albert had watched the puppy bound away. Cursing, he was trying to figure out how to secure Rex and Delilah so he could go after it when he saw Eric bite hold of a woman's dress.

Horrified, and knowing it was going to cause another scene right before the police arrived, he was looking right at her when she turned around. She didn't see him, but he caught a good look at her face through the milling crowd.

"Oh, my, word. It's a woman!" Albert exclaimed, once again amazed by how the dogs had found the criminal. He was about to let Rex go when another face he knew appeared at the gate. This one was trying to get in and was easy to pick out because he was in uniform.

A little out of breath, Chief Inspector Quinn had refused to run at Wainwright's sluggish pace. The constable was half a street behind him, but Quinn was certain he would find Albert Smith here and nothing was going to stop him.

"Five pounds entry fee, please," said the woman on the turnstile when Quinn attempted to push by her.

"What? I'm the police. There's a wanted criminal in here. Let me in."

"It's all for charity," she added.

Huffing, Quinn felt for his wallet, remembered he didn't have any cash because no one uses it these days, and ran around to the exit where he intended to shove his way through.

Chrissy yanked her dress free, sending the pup tumbling, and made a run for the gate.

Chief Inspector Quinn saw a gap in the slow stream of visitors leaving, timed his move, and darted for the gap.

He barrelled into Chrissy, knocking her backward and grabbing onto her so she wouldn't fall.

Eric, back on his paws, was bounding uncoordinatedly after his quarry and arrived behind her feet just in time to trip her and the police officer now clinging to her. They both went down, scaring Eric sufficiently that he chose to run back to the safety of his mum and dad.

Slamming into the ground with the cop on top of her, Chrissy's gun skittered free and Chief Inspector Quinn's ears informed his brain that he knew precisely what the sound was.

Partially trapped beneath the police officer's body even as he tried to extricate himself and apologise, she made a grab for the gun.

He got there first.

"I believe I will keep hold of this, Miss. You are under arrest." Quinn desperately wanted to explore the grounds for Albert Smith, but he would be derelict in his duty if he didn't deal with an armed woman first.

Taking out his handcuffs, he cast his eyes quickly around in the hope that Albert Smith might be somewhere in sight, but he wasn't.

The Contest

U nable to believe his bad luck, Albert had ducked back inside the marquee. He'd missed something happening inside, that had been obvious from all the cheering, clapping, and laughing that erupted while he was outside, but his eyes almost popped out of his head when he saw the devastation.

To start with, the neat rows of contestants were now in utter disarray, and to a person they were covered in Eton Mess. Behind them the walls of the marquee were splattered with cream and pieces of strawberry. It wasn't just them though. Edwina was coated in white goo too, plus at least one of the judges.

The bigger news was that the crazy gunman in the sheepskin coat was out cold on the ground and being tended to by a pair of St John's Ambulance Brigade medics. They were carefully loading him onto a stretcher and when they lifted him, Albert saw that his hands were tied.

The audience inside the marquee was applauding, not that Albert was sure which bit they were most pleased about.

He'd only been outside for a few minutes.

In the middle of the marquee, a local reporter, assigned to the factory open day for the seventh year in a row, felt like he had won the lottery. This was going to make the front cover! He was sure he'd managed to get some action shots as the puddings flew, but there was no time to check his camera, because the drama wasn't over yet.

Mr Barrowman, standing in for the firm's chief executive who had allegedly been called away for urgent family business, had elected to storm off. Covered in Eton Mess, he didn't wish to be photographed for the paper.

A new person had stepped up to take over, a woman this time called Bella Marsh. She was at the front of the dais now to address the audience and contestants.

"It would appear that we only have one entry left," she looked from Melissa where she stood like an island in the middle of the marquee to the rest of the competitors in their shambled state. Where previously all were standing neatly behind their tables, now they were clumped in groups or starting to pack possessions back into their bags.

"Is there anyone else with a pudding, or even part of a pudding they can present to the judges?" Bella enquired, loving the sound of her voice coming through the address system.

Melissa stared at the contestants. A few of them were eyeing the remains of their dishes, but against her four pristine puddings in their presentation glasses, they knew they didn't stand a chance. Elation bloomed until she heard someone call out from behind her.

Albert, lurking at the back of the marquee and certain he was to be arrested in the next few minutes, was choosing to go out on top. The awful and unpleasant Melissa Medina, who he'd met only because he was trying to selflessly ensure her safety, wasn't going to have it all her own way.

Threading Delilah's lead through Rex and Eric's collar, he tied all three dogs to one of the marquee's steel uprights and made his way through the audience.

"Excuse me. Pardon me. Sorry, can I just get through." At the barrier keeping the audience at bay, Albert swung a leg over and with a helping hand hopped into the open centre of the marquee. Announcing loudly, he said, "I have something I can present to the judges."

Bella spoke into the microphone. "I'm sorry, sir. The competition is only open to those who registered to take part."

Passing Melissa, Albert tipped her a wink and called out. "I am registered. This is my table here." He pointed to one that had less mess on it than any other and the mess that was there was only due to the food fight.

"Well," Bella made sure to smile for the audience. "It would seem we do still have a contest." She began clapping, encouraging the crowd to join her, which they did.

From his refrigerator, Albert plucked the box he'd bought at the bakery and placing it on the floor he withdrew the four Eton Mess puddings he'd purchased. Arranging them on a glass dish Jessica took from her gran's cupboard, Albert balanced it on one hand and rose to his feet.

"He's cheating!" Melissa protested loudly. "He made them before he came here! My table is next to his and he's been absent the whole time."

Unwilling to lie, Albert confessed, "I didn't make them at all. I bought them at the bakery across the street. Do they still qualify as a legitimate entry?"

Melissa snapped, "Of course they don't!" but the judges had already gone into a huddle, their heads together. "Do they?" she asked incredulously.

Like many other people who met Melissa, the judges were not fans and though the old man with the bought puddings was operating way outside of the rules, they saw an opportunity to really stick it to a woman they all loathed.

"We're going to allow it," the head judge announced.

Melissa's cry of, "What!" was drowned in the roar of cheering and applause from a crowd that were still coming down from the frenzied high of watching the food fight.

Bella called for quiet and invited both contestants to present their puddings. The sound of multiple police squad cars arriving at the gates was unmistakable, but no one inside the marquee was going to tear themselves away now even if they were curious to find out what was going on outside.

Equals yet Rivals

J ust inside the factory main gates, Chief Inspector Quinn waved to attract attention. A line of squad cars were queuing outside and making it very obvious they wanted to be let in.

Quinn bellowed. "Open the gates!"

Two cars back, Chief Inspector Murdo was squinting through his screen. "Quinn," he remarked. "How the heck did he get here first?"

Quinn barked at the crowds until they parted and waved the cars in through the gates, automatically taking charge as he always did. Wainwright had finally arrived just before the squad cars. He was sweating despite the cool air and heaving to get some oxygen back in his lungs, but Quinn handed over the suspect and left him to manage her.

Pointing and directing, Quinn made his voice the loudest around. Until Chief Inspector Murdo stepped from his car.

"Thank you, Ian," he nodded to his old friend from the academy. "I have it from here."

Quinn was first on scene and had been promoted to chief inspector a full year earlier than the man now looking to take over. "But ..."

"I have it from here, Ian," Graham Murdo repeated more forcefully. "This is my area, and these are my officers. I thank you for your assistance." Murdo nodded his head at the woman in cuffs. "Is she the one responsible for the body in the factory?"

Quinn failed to hide his confusion.

Murdo's sergeant had already deployed in the direction of the main factory building taking four uniformed officers with her and Murdo intended to follow.

Explaining to his bewildered equal, Murdo said, "We received reports of shots fired from local residents."

"Yes. I heard them myself. This woman," he pointed at Chrissy, "was carrying a firearm which has recently been discharged."

Murdo's forehead creased a little. "Then there's more than one person here with a gun. I have a report of another man in the marquee. He's been disarmed too." Shifting his gaze to pin two of his officers in place, he barked, "Hayes, Lewis, with me." To Quinn, "I'm going there now. You can put the woman you have in custody in the back of my car. Baker will take her from your man."

"I'll come with you," Quinn started moving and met with the palm of Murdo's hand.

"No, Ian. Like I said, I thank you for your assistance. I will be sure to have my boss call your boss to make it clear you were first on scene and took one of the armed suspects single-handedly. However," Graham moved to block Quinn's path and was sure to keep eye contact, "I know your penchant for claiming glory. This is my bust. You can wait by the cars."

"No, you don't understand," Quinn grabbed Murdo's forearm, only letting it go when Graham jinked an eyebrow in warning. "I am pursuing a man connected to the explosion in Whitstable. There's a distinct possibility that he is here right now. You need to close the gates and keep everyone here. Then I need to use your officers to search for him."

Doing nothing to hide his doubt, Murdo argued, "What makes you think the man you want is here of all places? If he's on the run, a day out at a factory open day is hardly the thing to do."

"Because of the Gastrothief," Quinn snapped too quickly, only realising once the words were out that he'd introduced a subject he was now going to have to explain.

Murdo's expression demanded Quinn keep going.

Sighing in an exhausted manner, Quinn tried to explain. "The man I'm pursuing ... he's a former detective superintendent. He's got three kids who are all senior detectives in the Met, and he's been using them to conduct a secret private investigation into a character he refers to as the Gastrothief."

Murdo, tolerating Quinn, but feeling like his patience was being tested, asked, "This man, if his kids are senior officers, how old is he?"

"Seventy-eight," Quinn admitted reluctantly.

A laugh burst from Murdo's lips. "A seventy-eight-year-old man? That's who you're pursuing? That's priceless. Stay here, Ian. I have a dead body and at least one more gunman to deal with. My officers are going to quickly and quietly shut down the open day and evacuate the premises. If you want to watch the exit, you can shout out if you spot the man you are after." Walking away, Quinn heard it when Murdo chuckled again, "The Gastrothief. That's a good one."

Fuming, Quinn watched as Chief Inspector Murdo, flanked by two officers, headed for the marquee.

And the Winner is

...

The judges inspected, tasted, tested, and compared the two sets of Eton Mess puddings. Ultimately though, they had picked their winner before they even saw what Albert had to show them.

Melissa watched, her eyes narrowed, and her comments kept to herself though inside she was thinking murderous thoughts. How dare they fiddle the rules to include the readymade puddings her opponent had brought with him.

The head judge wrote their answer on a slip of paper and handed it to Bella.

Making a show of unfolding it, Bella Marsh lifted her eyes to look around the packed marquee.

"It would appear we have a unanimous decision, ladies and gentlemen."

The reporter lifted his camera and got ready to snap the winner's face, forever capturing the emotion brought by victory.

"This year's Eton Mess winner is ..." Bella paused for dramatic effect and watched as the crowd all leaned forward to hear, "Albert Smith!"

Melissa's horrified cry was drowned out by the eruption of cheering, and though she spat a foul comment in Albert's direction before she stormed from the marquee, he didn't hear it. He was too busy reeling from the photographer snapping pictures of his face. Albert had failed to think through the consequences of winning. His photograph would be in the paper. Okay, it was a local rag with a minimal readership. Nevertheless, it was a poor tactic for a person trying to fly under the radar.

The head judge, her blouse stained where the Eton Mess hit it, came forward to shake his hand, a queue quickly forming as the rest of the judges, Bella, and a goodly portion of the competitors came forward to congratulate the winner.

Chief Inspector Murdo entered the marquee in time to hear the winner being announced. The name 'Albert Smith' meant nothing to him which was ironic for had Quinn thought to once name the man he was after, Murdo would have called his old pal in to confirm it was the right person.

Looking around, Murdo saw the state of the competition area and the people in it. There were blobs of cream everywhere. He'd never been to the open day before, but made a mental note to not be on duty next year. If it drew this many people who cheered this hard it had to be worth attending.

Focusing on what he was supposed to be doing, he looked around for anyone who might be in charge. Working his way to the dais by going around the back of the audience, Murdo reached the people there and was directed to speak with Bella.

Now effectively running the firm in her head, Bella was only too happy to be identified as the person of authority.

"Yes, he's with a pair of St John's Ambulance medics. We had them here for the day in case they were needed. They are tucked out of sight behind the dais. He's tied up and one of the competitors is ex-army, he made the weapon safe and is back there with him too."

As Bella led the cops away, Albert allowed his heart to beat again. Surrounded by people and still being applauded, he'd spotted the all too familiar uniforms and figured they were here to arrest him. He'd been blurting his name and writing it on entry forms and the like all day, so it was going to be no shock when Chief Inspector Quinn tracked him down.

Now they were heading around the back of the dais to the admin area it hid.

Breathing a sigh of relief, he jumped when a hand closed around his left bicep.

"Albert," Jessica hissed at him, "we need to get you out of here. Come on." Pulling him away from the partying, pudding-covered competitors, she asked, "Where are the dogs?"

Quinn's Moment

In front of Constable Wainwright, Chief Inspector Quinn acted as if everything was proceeding according to his plan. Inside, he continued to seethe.

Unused to taking orders or being shoved into a backseat position, he tolerated it for a couple of minutes, but that was enough.

Stiffening the muscles in his back so he stood just that little bit taller, Ian Quinn was about to march his way into the marquee when he heard a radio crackle and Chief Inspector Murdo's voice filled the air.

It was coming over Constable Baker's radio, the junior officer Murdo had left to mind the cars and the woman Quinn arrested.

"Baker, is there an ambulance out there anywhere? The suspect here is unconscious, and the St John's guys aren't really equipped to help."

Quinn jerked his head around to check the gate in time to see an ambulance pulling up to the gates.

He shouted, "Let them in!" and jogged over to direct where they parked. To Baker he barked, "Advise your boss you will escort them to his location and confirm where he is."

The paramedics, both men in their thirties, clocked Quinn – he was hard to miss standing right in their path – and followed where he showed them to go.

Quinn saw the men exchange a silent glance before getting out and was waiting impatiently for them to unload the gurney from the rear of their vehicle. What he did not see was the armed woman he arrested thumping urgently on the rear window of the squad car she was locked inside.

Chrissy's hands were cuffed, necessitating she use both fists as one, but neither Vlad nor Niki saw her, for their attention was on the senior police officer demanding they hurry themselves. They were trapped now and no doubt hoping they could bluff their way through the situation.

Quinn wanted to get into the marquee to look for Albert Smith. If the old man was anywhere, then he was in there, Quinn could feel it in his blood, and that meant every moment he wasted outside was another chance for his quarry to escape.

Hurrying the paramedics along, he said, "This is a live and potentially dangerous situation still, chaps. Keep your eyes peeled for this man."

He held up his phone, the screen of which now displayed Albert's Smith's face. "He looks old and harmless, but is linked to the explosion in Whitstable two nights ago and may be involved in terrorist activities."

Quinn didn't believe anything of the sort, but he wanted the paramedics to act as additional eyes and ears.

Expecting a reaction from them, Chief Inspector Quinn thought it curious that neither man questioned if it was safe or what to do if they did spot the suspect.

Inside the marquee, the applause Quinn heard had died away and people were starting to leave. Forced to raise his voice to clear a passage, his uniform did the rest so the paramedics with their gurney on wheels could get through.

At the edge of the barrier on the entrance side of the marquee, Quinn stopped, his eyes narrowed to slits as he gazed around the open space. From person to person, he checked and rejected one after the other until he accepted that Albert Smith simply wasn't here.

Turning about, he was shocked to find the paramedics were still behind him, seemingly waiting silently for his next instruction.

"Where's the girl, then?" one of the men asked.

Quinn frowned. "Girl? What Girl? You're here to collect an unconscious man, are you not?"

The second paramedic was quick to say, "Yes, that's right," smiling like it was funny. "We get so many shouts; they all kind of merge into one after a while."

His frown deepening, Quinn spat, "So what are you standing around for? The patient is over there," he shot an arm toward the dais and the hidden admin area beyond.

Curious, Chief Inspector Quinn followed the paramedics as they hustled through the marquee. It was thinning out now, the contest – whatever it had been – clearly over, and both the audience and competitors were heading for the exit.

At the dais, Quinn watched the paramedics collapse the gurney so it came down to floor level. Murdo was facing away from him, but one of his constables murmured something and nodded his head in Quinn's direction.

He was vaguely aware of Murdo spinning around and snapping a comment in his direction, but Quinn was too absorbed watching the chaps from the ambulance to pay the local commander any attention.

"Did you hear what I said?" Graham Murdo growled, closing the gap between them.

Quinn didn't answer. The paramedics were getting ready to cross load their patient from one stretcher to the next, but they hadn't checked his vitals or performed any basic inspection to confirm he was even safe to move.

Chief Inspector Murdo got into Quinn's face, blocking his view and almost blew a gasket when Quinn darted to one side to look around him.

"What the devil!"

Ignoring Murdo, Quinn addressed the paramedics when he politely asked, "What's the patient's blood pressure now?"

The paramedics exchanged a glance, their faces hidden from view as they knelt over the unconscious form.

Less than two yards from them, Quinn saw when they made their decision and released a grunt of exertion when he shoved Murdo out of the way.

Both men were spinning around and pulling something from inside their clothing. Quinn had already figured out that they were not genuine, and it didn't require a lot of brain power to make the leap from there to 'probably dangerous'.

As Vlad and Niki's weapons cleared the holsters tucked deep inside their paramedic's uniform, Quinn bellowed, "Gun!" and threw himself at the imposters.

On the other side of the curtain erected to hide the admin area from sight, the reporter from the Eton Mail ran the video function on his camera. He'd been chased away twice already, but in his book a good journalist never pays attention to the rules.

The other cops were responding, all save for Chief Inspector Murdo who was thrown off balance by Chief Inspector Quinn and was unable to correct himself in time.

A gun went off, the sound loud for those who were close to it, and it happened in the instant before Quinn's body slammed into the fake paramedics. It missed him by such a small margin that its passing crisped the material of his tunic.

The next day, when the footage was all over the internet and Quinn was being hailed as a hero cop shortlisted for a medal, all Ian Quinn could think about was the other article the Eton Mess journalist published.

The picture of Albert Smith holding the Eton Mess trophy burned into his brain. He'd been so close.

Goodbyes

Two minutes after leaving the marquee by slipping back under the canvas at the back, and blithely unaware of what was about to happen inside, Albert was reunited with Rex. Edwina, Jessica, Delilah, and Eric were with them.

Leading the group, Jessica said, "I can get you out through the staff carpark. We'll have to go the long way around to get home, but once we've got your suitcase, I think we should get you to the train station. That's if you still want to go to Cornwall. You're serious about catching this Gastrothief, aren't you?"

Albert nodded his head slowly.

"Yes, I am."

At a gate in a chain link fence, Jessica punched a code into a keypad. A solenoid clicked and the door unlocked.

Albert's legs were already tired – he'd put in some mileage today and a chunk of it had been running. His hips were aching, and his feet were sore, but he kept those details to himself.

Avoiding the police at the front of the factory added half a mile or more onto the journey, but they arrived back at Edwina's house soon enough.

"You can stay the night if you like," Edwina offered, her eyes twinkling again.

"Gran, he needs to get to Cornwall," Jessica reminded her.

Albert offered her a smile, but said, "Honestly, there's too much chance Chief Inspector Quinn will speak to someone who will identify the two of you as being in my company today. The last thing you want is for the police to find me here."

Jessica paused at the foot of the stairs. "Is everything in your suitcase, or do you need to pack?"

"It's all ready to go," Albert assured her.

While Jessica went to fetch Albert's suitcase from the spare room, Albert thought about his day, about how wrong he had been and how much he'd underestimated Chief Inspector Quinn. He might believe the man was a fool, but Albert couldn't deny his determination.

"A cup of tea before you go?" Edwina wandered through to her kitchen.

Albert followed, but asked, "Got anything stronger?" A memory surfaced, and he followed his question with "Sorry, no, Jessica told me there's no alcohol in the house."

Edwina cackled. "Is that what she told you?" Reaching into a cupboard, Edwina removed a large box of cornflakes from which she extracted a half full bottle of whisky.

The dogs had gravitated toward the kitchen with the humans, and it was there that Rex cornered Delilah and chose to voice his thoughts.

"It looks like I'm leaving shortly," Rex pointed out to Delilah. "Maybe the two of us could ..."

Unexpectedly, Delilah growled in his face, "Could what? You dogs are all the same. Nothing in your heads but mating." All the friendliness was gone and in its place was unexplained aggression.

Seeing the exchange and reading it for what it was, Edwina cackled yet again.

"I shouldn't bother, Rex," she patted him on the shoulder. "Her season has ended. She's no use for you now."

He'd already backed away a pace, concerned Delilah might snap at him, and now Rex understood the sudden change in attitude. He'd met other bitches in his life, and they were all like this, their behaviour changeable and bizarre from a dog's perspective.

Eric came to Rex's side. "What's going on, Daddy? Did I hear you say that you were leaving?"

Rex felt a genuine tug at his heart when he looked down at the pup. He had no connection to Eric, no blood attachment, but it felt like he was the pup's father all the same.

"That's right, kid, but listen, you need to enrol for the police dog academy. You're a natural for it."

"Really?" Eric's tail wagged. "Do you think I could be like you?"

"Better than me," Rex assured him. "Just try not to make the humans look too bad. They don't like it when you do that."

Eric nuzzled into Rex's neck, enjoying the warmth and security he felt around the bigger dog.

Above them, Albert watched the pup and an idea formed.

"Have you decided what you are going to do with Eric?"

Edwina looked up from her tumbler of dark liquid.

"Hmm? Oh, yes. Well, like I said before, I can't really sell him, and I don't like the idea of dropping him off at a shelter for rehoming."

"Have you thought about giving him to the police?"

Edwina looked at Albert and then down at her puppy.

"You mean like for police dog work? Would they take him?"

Albert chuckled. "Absolutely. They are always looking for the next tranche of healthy young dogs to train. He's a little older than most pups, but I can get a message to my son. He knows who to talk to.

They'll take him if it's something you want. I saw him chase down that woman who dressed up to look like a man. I think he might have a natural ability."

Edwina pursed her lips, watching Eric play fighting with Rex.

"I'll think about it."

Jessica reappeared, Albert's suitcase in her right hand. She placed it on the floor.

"I just got off the phone with my editor at the paper. You won't believe what was in those files."

Her statement required expanding on, and she was only too happy to do so. Over the next few minutes, while on the floor between them Rex wrestled playfully with Eric, Jessica explained about the long history of chemical deliveries coming to the Eton Mess factory. The Environment Agency had agents already gearing up to hit Wallace's. They weren't going to wait until the morning, they would arrive tonight, and the place would be torn apart.

It was possible that there was no one else at the firm involved, only the CEO, Oliver Walsh. The inventory of shipments wasn't exactly documented, but the trail was there. The bigger news was what else the files contained.

Hidden in a different subset of folders was a money laundering system that appeared to be a small part of a larger network. It was managed within the firm's pension fund with the money being paid to non-existent or deceased employees.

"It's quite genius," Jessica remarked before doing her best to explain how it was that the computer tech whizzes at her firm had been able to trace the author of the files. "It was a man called Percy Crumley. And that's who gran knocked out with an Eton Mess this afternoon."

"Two Eton Messes," Edwina corrected her. "It took me two," she said with a chuckle.

"They sent me a picture of him. It had to be more than a decade old, but it was the crazy guy who chased us through the factory."

"What about the other two?" Edwina asked. "The giant in the suit and the woman who dressed like a man?"

Jessica shrugged. "That I don't know, but Percy Crumley has a record as long as your arm and connections to organised crime."

"Lackies," Albert offered his opinion. "Probably. Paid hitmen. Crumley must have sent them and then followed up when they weren't quick enough or something." He finished the glass of neat whisky, downing the last of it and pulling a face as it burned down through his body in a pleasing way. Handing the empty glass to Edwina, he said, "I really ought to be going. If I don't shift my backside soon, I'll not have enough time to reach Cornwall tonight."

"I'll drive you," Jessica offered.

Albert picked up his suitcase. "Thanks. We'd better go to the next station along the line. There's likely to be police at the one for Eton."

"No," Jessica jangled her car keys. "I mean I'll drive you to Cornwall. It's not that far."

Albert's eyebrows rose. "It's got to be two hundred miles."

"A hundred and eighty-five according to my phone. It won't take long. I'll be back before midnight, and I can be on the phone talking to my people at the paper the whole time. They need a report from me, and I can dictate it."

Albert's natural inclination was to argue; he wasn't used to people putting themselves out for him, but instead he dipped his head in acceptance and appreciation.

Later, settled into the passenger seat of Jessica's car as it ate up the miles, Albert thought about the Gastrothief. Rex was snoring on the backseat, lying upside down with his top lips obeying gravity to show his teeth.

Jessica was talking to a bunch of people at her paper. They were overjoyed at what she had given them; it wasn't just a major scoop, it was two!

He wasn't listening to her conversation though; he was thinking about Cornwall and about when his journey might be over. Until today, he hadn't realised how much he wanted to go home. His little jaunt around the British Isles might have gone on and on because until a few days ago he could have gone home at any point and didn't want to. Now that he couldn't, his stance had changed.

It wasn't homesickness exactly, but it was something. He'd gone to Eton believing he might find the evidence he needed. Had he done so, the police would have taken over and a taskforce would be taking a serious look at the same list of connected crimes Albert knew would lead them to find the person behind it all.

As he drifted off to sleep, he questioned whether he would have more luck in Cornwall.

Epilogue — Two Weeks Later

Sergeant Gruber looked along the line at his new recruits. The German Shepherd puppies were far from what you would call inspiring, but that was how it always was. They started out as dopey furballs and six months of training later, they were slick, obedient K9 police dogs.

Usually they came from working dog kennels and began their socialisation and training when just a few weeks old, but somehow he had a dog that was almost five months. Someone had pulled some strings somewhere; not that it mattered to Charlie Gruber. A dog was a dog to him. The giant lump, three times bigger than any of the other recruits, would either pass or fail.

There was something about him though. Something about the way the dog closed his eyes when he sniffed the air and how he watched the handlers as if assessing them, not the other way around.

There had been another dog like that a few years ago. Charlie strained his head to make the name appear, but it wouldn't come. Curious now, he crossed to an old metal filing cabinet – one day they would get some budget and be able to have their records digitally stored.

It took a few minutes, but he found the file he was looking for.

"Rex Harrison," he read the name aloud with a wry smile pulling at his facial muscles. "God, what a pain that dog was." Too talented and too intelligent by far, Rex Harrison's problem, so far as all the handlers were concerned, was that he believed he was cleverer than they were.

Charlie joked at the time that Rex was probably right, but his subordinates didn't find the joke very funny.

Putting the file away, he went back to the dog and crouched to pet him.

"What are you going to be like, eh? Are you going to be a problem like Rex Harrison was? Or are you going to be a good boy?" Charlie lifted the dog's tag and read the name on it. "Eric. That's not a bad name actually. We need a theme for this intake. Maybe I'll go for stars of British TV. You can be Eric Morecambe." He angled his arm to the next dog in line. "And you can be Ernie Wise."

Charlie returned to his desk where he had a pad of sticky notes. He wrote the names of twenty old British TV stars and stuck them to the wall behind each dog's kennel.

Clapping his hands together to get the attention of the dogs and their handlers, Sergeant Gruber said, "Right. Today is day one of training and we always start day one with take down practice." It had long been tradition to start the dogs' training by having them chase a man in a padded suit. It was fun for everyone, not least because the pups were always terrible at it and often the whole lot of them ran away in terror.

The pups listened to the human talking but none of them had any idea what he was saying.

Apart from one.

Eric's tail wagged as he yipped, "Oh, yeah! My dad told me all about this. He called it chase and bite and he said to always go for the soft bits that aren't padded. He said it's much better training that way and the humans learn to run faster which makes it more realistic."

Charlie Gruber glanced at the yipping pup and wondered again if they were going to have a problem.

The End

Author's Notes:

Hello, Dear Reader,

It's close to midnight on a Sunday as I finish this book. I have a nibble of chocolate and a G&T as my reward. My family is asleep upstairs where it is probably warmer than they want it, for the UK is in the grip of a heat wave. We don't get many of them, not like this at least. My garden looks like scorched earth and the paddling pool is getting a lot of use.

This story proved harder to write than I expected and that was all to do with opening a small publishing firm. Setting up a new business takes a lot of work, as anyone who has ever done it will testify. Many of the necessary tasks are those you have not taken into account before you started, but now that I am largely over those hurdles, and the machine is in place, I can get back to the words.

Over the last few years, I have churned out what some consider to be a lot of books. Whether they are right or not could be debated for hours, but I have achieved what I have by writing continuously. It is easier for me to do it that way and I find myself 'inside' the story in a manner that allows the words to flow.

Because in recent weeks I have had to stop writing to do other things, the words, when I was writing, came much slower. To prove my point, I cleared my desk three days ago and forced myself to do nothing but finish this book. I wrote more than a third of it in that period.

The Albert and Rex story has just three episodes remaining. I will finish at book fifteen, but fear not for it will only be the end of their British adventure. Next year I will start them on a new trip, this time in Europe where they will visit a plethora of major cities to sample their famous dishes.

I cannot wait to get started.

If I live long enough, I hope to write forty-five Albert and Rex books across three series. Right now that feels a little daunting and I have a stack of other series and projects to fit in too. We will see how it goes.

I mention St John's Ambulance in this book and suspect that it might not mean anything in some parts of the world. It is a volunteer organisation for children and adults to learn and practice first aid. That training is then put to good use at events where having medics on standby is desirable. The equipment, the first aid supplies and even the ambulances come from charitable donations, money from the Ministry of Health and from the Accident Compensation Corporation. In my teenage years, I was a volunteer with them.

I also mention Eric Morecambe and Ernie Wise who in Britain are considered to be TV gods from a golden era. In the seventies and eighties, it wasn't possible to get through Christmas without their big TV special. Even now they are shown regularly. They even made a few low budget, but acceptable movies.

It feels like bedtime now, so I'll end things here and thank you for reading this far. If you want to make an Eton Mess of your own, there's a recipe over the page and it really is quite easy.

Take care.

Steve Higgs

Recipe

Ingredients

- 600g/1lb 5oz strawberries, hulled

- 2 tbsp icing sugar

- 600ml/20fl oz double cream

- 200g/7oz seasonal berries (such as raspberries, cherries, currants, or more strawberries)

- 5 readymade meringue nests or 1 batch of the homemade meringues

For the homemade meringues

- 2 large egg whites

- 120g/4¼oz caster sugar

- ¼ tsp vanilla extract

Method

1. If you are using homemade meringues, make these first. Pre-heat your oven to 110C/100C Fan/Gas ¼ and line a baking sheet with non-stick baking paper.

2. Put the egg whites into a clean mixing bowl and beat with an electric whisk until stiff peaks form when you lift out the whisk. Whisk in the caster sugar, one tablespoon at a time, until the mixture is really thick, glossy and will hold in a stiff peak. Briefly whisk in the vanilla.

3. Place 5 large dollops of the meringue on the prepared baking sheet, leaving space in between. Bake on the lowest shelf of your oven for an hour, or until the meringues easily peel away from the paper. Cool and keep in an airtight container for up to 3 days before using.

4. For the mess, put 150g/5½oz of the strawberries into a blender or food processor with ½ tablespoon of the icing sugar. Pulse to form a smooth purée. Halve or quarter the remaining strawberries into bite-size pieces.

5. Whip the double cream and remaining 1½ tablespoon of icing sugar together until soft peaks form when you remove the whisk (they should almost hold their shape).

6. To assemble, crumble 4 of the meringues and add to the cream along with all the berries. Fold in lightly, then very briefly stir in the strawberry purée to make swirls in the cream (as you spoon the mess into bowls it will ripple more). Divide between 6 bowls or glasses, crush the final meringue over the top and eat immediately.

Recipe Tips

1.   It's important to use a clean bowl when making meringues because any grease will prevent the egg whites from forming the necessary stiff peaks. If in doubt, you can wipe your bowl with a little lemon juice and kitchen paper.

2.   Both the purée and cream can be chilled for a few hours in advance – just make sure you don't over-whip the cream as it will firm up even more in the fridge.

3.   Once assembled the mess should be eaten straight away – the meringue will soften and become chewy rather than crisp if left sitting in the cream.

History of the Dish

E ton Mess is a traditional English dessert consisting of a mixture of strawberries or other berries, meringue, and whipped cream. First mentioned in print in 1893, it is commonly believed to originate from Eton College and is served at the annual cricket match against the pupils of Harrow School. Eton Mess is occasionally served at Harrow School, where it is referred to as Harrow mess.

Eton Mess was served in the 1930s in the school's "sock shop" (tuck shop) and was originally made with either strawberries or bananas mixed with ice-cream or cream. Meringue was a later addition. An Eton Mess can be made with many other types of summer fruit, but strawberries are regarded as more traditional.

The word mess may refer to the appearance of the dish or may be used in the sense of "a quantity of food", particularly "a prepared dish of soft food" or "a mixture of ingredients cooked or eaten together".

ETON MESS MASSACRE

In recent times, "Eton Mess" has often been used by commentators in the media to describe political infighting within the UK over issues such as Brexit. Eton Mess is used because a number of Conservative politicians were educated at Eton College.

What's Next for Albert and Rex?

Cornish Pasty Conspiracy

F ollowing a trail of clues to a sleepy seaside village in the southwest corner of England, retired police detective, Albert Smith, aims to prove his theory of a master criminal by catching the 'Gastrothief's' agents red-handed.

With trusted former police dog, Rex Harrison at his side, the crime-busting duo know precisely who and what to look for.

However, beneath the narrow streets of the picturesque resort a far more sinister plot is being hatched and if Albert were to look over his shoulder, he might notice a set of eyes lurking in his shadow.

ETON MESS MASSACRE

He is being hunted.

To the backdrop of a cider and pasty festival, man and dog must risk it all save that which makes Britain great.

Baking. It can get a guy killed.

More Books By Steve Higgs

About the Author

At school, the author was mostly disinterested in every subject except creative writing, for which, at age ten, he won his first award. However, calling it his first award suggests that there have been more, which there have not. Accolades may come but, in the meantime, he is having a ball writing mystery stories and crime thrillers and claims to have more than a hundred books forming an unruly queue in his head as they clamour to get out. He lives in the south-east corner of England with a duo of lazy sausage dogs. Surrounded by rolling hills, brooding castles, and vineyards, he doubts he will ever leave, the beer is just too good.

Printed in the USA
CPSIA information can be obtained
at www.ICGtesting.com
LVHW021643080224
771080LV00013B/663